B.5 T 2.28

BALLET
SHOES

BALLET
SHOES

NOEL STREATFEILD

A YEARLING BOOK

Published by
Dell Publishing Co., Inc.
1 Dag Hammarskjold Plaza
New York, New York 10017

Yearling ® TM 913705, Dell Publishing Co., Inc.

ISBN: 0-440-41508-X

Reprinted by arrangement with Random House, Inc.
Printed in the United States of America
Seventh Dell printing—December 1983

CW

CONTENTS

About the Three in This Book

*

Pauline, Petrova and Posy Fossil are not really sisters, but they have been brought up together like one family.

When they were still quite little, their guardian got poor. Somebody suggested that even children can help when people are poor, and they were sent to the Academy of Dancing and Stage Training.

No child is allowed to appear on the stage in England until he or she is twelve, and then only with a license. Pauline was, of course, the first to be twelve, and she had a busy time. First she was "Alice" in "Alice in Wonderland", and she finished up as the eldest Prince in "Richard the Third", and after that she went into films. Pauline is in Hollywood now.

Petrova was not twelve until nearly two years after Pauline; she was not a success; she did play "Mustardseed" in "A Midsummer Night's Dream", but those were the only words she spoke on the stage. She walked on, or danced in a troupe after that. She never cared. She hated acting; her heart was in the air. Look out for Petrova; one day her name may be famous.

Posy never had a license. She won't be twelve until next September. If you are a balletomane, watch for Posy; dancers such as she is are not born every day.

Noel Streatfeild

July, 1936.

I

Great-Uncle Matthew
and His Fossils

*

THE Fossil sisters lived in the Cromwell Road. At
that end of it which is farthest away from the Bromp-
ton Road, and yet sufficiently near it so one could be
taken to look at the dolls' houses in the Victoria and
Albert every wet day. If the weather were not too wet,
one was expected to "save the penny and walk."

Saving the penny and walking was a great feature
of their lives.

"Gum," Pauline, the eldest, would say, "must have
been a very taxi person; he couldn't have ever thought
about walking or he'd never have bought a house at the
far end of the longest road in London."

"I expect," Petrova, the second, would argue, "he
had a motor-car all his own, and he never hired anything."

G.U.M. was the quick way of saying Great-Uncle
Matthew. He was a legendary figure to the children,
as he had gone on a voyage, and not come back, before
any of them were old enough to remember him clearly.

He had, however, been of the utmost importance in their lives.

"He's been," Pauline once said, "like the stork in the fairy-tale. He very nearly did bring us in his beak." Storks in the Fossil children's nursery were always called Gums after that.

Gum had been a very important person. He had collected some of the finest fossils in the world, and though to many people fossils may not seem to be very interesting things to collect, there are others who find them as absorbing as sensible collections, such as stamps. Collecting fossils, he naturally needed somewhere to put them, and that is how he came to buy the house in the Cromwell Road. It had large rooms, and about six floors, including the basement, and on every floor, and in almost every room, he kept fossils. Naturally a house like that needed somebody to look after it, and he found just the right person. Gum had one nephew, who had died leaving a widow and a little girl. What was more suitable than to invite the widow and her child Sylvia, and Nana her nurse, to live in the house and take care of it for him? Ten years later the widowed niece died, but by then his great-niece Sylvia was sixteen, so she, helped by Nana, took her mother's place, and saw that the house and the fossils were all right.

Sometimes when the house got too full Nana would say:

"Now, Miss Sylvia dear, you must tell your uncle not another fossil until a few have gone out of the door."

Sylvia hated saying this, but she was far too much in awe of Nana to do anything else. Terrible upsets were the result. First Gum said no fossil would leave the house except over his dead body. Then, when he'd toned down a little and realized some had to go, in spite of his body being anything but dead, he would collect a few small, rather bad specimens and give them away. Then, after a day or two, during which he mooned round the house under Nana's stern eyes and Sylvia's rather sorry ones, a notice would suddenly appear in *The Times,* to say that Professor Matthew Brown had given another generous gift of fossils to a museum. That meant that men would come with packing-cases and take some of the most important (which often meant the largest) fossils away. Nana would settle down with a sigh of contentment to cleaning those places where the fossils had stood, and Sylvia would comfort Gum by listening to his descriptions of where he was going to look for some more.

It was while looking for some more that the accident happened which put an end to Gum's fossil-hunting forever. He had climbed a mountain after a particular specimen, and he slipped and fell hundreds of feet, and crushed his leg so badly that he had to have it taken off.

You would have thought that a man who lived for nothing but fossils would have felt that there was nothing left to do when he couldn't go and look for them any more, but Gum wasn't that sort of man.

"I have traveled a lot on land, my dear," he said to Sylvia, "but very little by sea. Now I shall really see the world. And maybe I'll be finding something interesting to bring back."

"There's no need to do that, sir," Nana broke in firmly. "The house is full enough as it is. We don't want a lot of carved elephants and that about the place."

"Carved elephants!" Gum gave Nana a scornful look. "The world is full of entrancements, woman, any of which I might bring home, and you talk to me of carved elephants!"

But Nana held her ground.

"All right, sir; I'm sure I'm pleased you should see these entrancements, as you call them, but you let them bide. We want nothing more in this house."

The entrancement that Gum actually brought home was Pauline.

The ship on which he was traveling struck an ice-berg, and all the passengers had to take to the boats. In the night one of the boats filled with water and the passengers were thrown into the sea. Gum's boat went to the rescue, but by the time it got there everybody was drowned except a baby who was lying on a lifebelt, cooing happily. Gum collected the baby and wrapped her in his coat, and when they were at last rescued by a liner and taken to England, tried to find out to whom she belonged. That was the trouble. Nobody knew for sure whose baby she was; there had been other babies on board, and three were missing. She must go to an orphanage for female orphans, said everybody; but Gum said "No" to that. Things he found went to the Cromwell Road. He had meant to bring Sylvia back a present. Now, what could be better than this? He fussed and fumed while the adoption papers were made out, then he tucked the baby into the crook of his left arm, took his shabby old hold-all in his right, and limping because of his game leg, walked to the railway station, and went home to London and the Cromwell Road.

Gum, to whom time meant very little indeed, was never able to remember that other people might not be expecting him when he turned up without a word of warning after being away for months. This time he opened his front door, put down his hold-all, and looked round for a suitable place to put the baby. Seeing nowhere but the hall table or the umbrella stand, he called rather angrily for Sylvia.

"Hi, Sylvia! Good gracious me, I keep a pack of women in this house and none of them are about when they are wanted."

Nana and Sylvia were upstairs marking some new sheets. Nana stopped working, her needle held up as though it were a magic wand which could command silence.

"Hark. Isn't that the Professor's voice?"

Sylvia harked, and in a moment was down the stair with Nana panting behind.

"Darling Gum, why didn't you let me know you were coming?"

Her uncle kissed her.

"Why should I waste a stamp? Look"—he pushed the baby into her arms—"I've brought you a present."

Sylvia pulled the shawl back from the bundle he handed her, and then looked round at Nana, and said in a startled but pleased whisper:

"A baby!"

"A baby!" Nana almost jumped the two last stairs and snatched the child from Sylvia. She turned and faced Gum. "Really, sir, I don't know what you'll be bringing to the house next. Who do you suppose has time to look after a baby?"

"I thought all women liked babies," Gum protested.

"That's as may be." Nana was pink with rage. "If Miss Sylvia has any sense she won't take it. . . ."

She broke off, because the baby gave a sudden coo which made her look at it for the first time. Her face changed and seemed to melt, and she began to make noises as everybody makes to babies. Then suddenly she looked up fiercely at Sylvia.

"Which rooms am I to have for my nurseries?"

Nana coming round like that of course settled the baby's fate. She was given Sylvia's old nurseries at the top of the house, Nana became her slave, and Sylvia loved doing things for her when she was allowed (which wasn't often) as Nana believed in "having my nurseries to myself." Cook and the parlormaid and housemaid considered her a figure of romance. "Might be anybody, even royalty, saved like that from the ravening waves," Cook would say at the kitchen meals, and the two other maids would sigh and agree with her.

There was some trouble over calling her Pauline. Sylvia chose the name, as she said Saint Paul was rescued from the sea, so it was suitable. Gum, however, wanted to call her after one of his pet fossils, but Nana refused to allow it.

"Babies in my nurseries, sir," she said firmly, "never have had outlandish names, and they're not starting now. Miss Sylvia has chosen Pauline, and it's a nice sensible name, and called after a blessed saint, and no other name is going to be used, if you will forgive me speaking plain, sir."

A year later Gum brought Sylvia a second baby. On his travels this time his leg had given him trouble, and he had been landed and put into a hospital. There he had made friends with a Russian, a shabby, depressed fellow who yet somehow conveyed the impression that he hadn't always been shabby and depressed, but had once worn gay uniforms and had swung laughing through the snow in his jingling sleigh amidst rows of bowing peasants. This man had left Russia during the revolution, and he and his wife had tried to train themselves to earn a living. They had not been a success as wage-earners, and the wife became ill and died, leaving a small baby. When the man Boris was going to die too, the nurses in the hospital were most concerned.

"What shall we do?" they said. "Because there is his little baby in the children's ward."

"Don't trouble about that," Gum had answered

airily. "We have one baby at home that I have adopted. We shall have another."

Sylvia called this baby Petrova, as she had to have a Russian name, and it sounded a bit like Peter, and Nana thought that if one child were called after an apostle the other should be.

Nana did not even talk about not taking the baby this time. There were the nurseries, and there was Pauline.

"Very nice for Pauline to have a companion," she said. Then she looked at Petrova, who was a dark, sallow baby, very different from the golden-haired, pink-and-white Pauline. "Let's hope this one has brains, for it's easy to see who's going to be Miss Plain in my nursery."

Although Nana was quite pleased to welcome Petrova, she spoke firmly to Gum.

"Now, sir, before you go away again, do get into your head this house is not a crèche. Two babies in the nursery is right and proper, and such as the best homes have a right to expect, but two is enough. Bring one more and I give notice, and then where'd you be, with you and Miss Sylvia knowing no more of babies than you do of hens?"

Perhaps it was fear of what Nana might say, but the last baby Gum did not deliver himself. He sent

her round by district messenger in a basket. With her
he sent a pair of ballet shoes and a letter. The letter
said:

"DEAR NIECE,

   "Here is yet another Fossil to add to those in my
nursery. This is the little daughter of a dancer. The
father has just died, and the poor young mother has
no time for babies, so I said I would have her. All her
mother had to give her child was the little pair of
shoes enclosed. I regret not to bring the child myself,
but today I ran into a friend with a yacht who is visit-
ing some strange islands. I am joining him, and expect
to be away some years. I have arranged for the bank to
see after money for you for the next five years, but
before then I shall be home.

                     "Your affectionate uncle,

                                    "MATTHEW.
   "P.S. Her name is Posy. Unfortunate, but true."

The sudden arrival of little Posy caused an upset
in the nursery. Nana it was who took in the basket, and
when Sylvia got in and went up to see the baby, she
found her crumpled and rather pink, lying face down-
wards on Nana's flannel-aproned knee. Nana was hold-

ing an enormous powder puff, and she looked up as Sylvia came in.

"This is too much, this is," she said severely.

She shook a spray of fuller's earth over the baby. Sylvia looked humble.

"I quite agree, Nana. But what are we to do? Here she is."

Nana looked angrily at Posy.

"It isn't right. Here we are with Pauline almost four, and Petrova sixteen months, and down you pop this little fly-by-night. Two's enough, I've always said. I told the Professor so perfectly plain. Who is she? That's another thing I'd like to know."

"Well, her name's Posy, and her mother is a dancer."

"Posy! With the other two called as nice as can be after the Holy Apostles, that's a foolish sort of name." Nana gave a snort of disgust, and then, in case the baby should feel hurt, added "Blessed lamb."

"Right." Sylvia turned to the door. "Now I know how you feel, I'll make other arrangements for her, perhaps an orphanage. . . ."

"Orphanage!" Nana's eyes positively blazed. She pulled a tiny vest over Posy's unprotesting little head. "Who's thinking of orphanages? The Professor's taken her, and here she stays. But no more, and that's my last word."

"Well, I don't suppose there can be any more for a bit," Sylvia said hopefully. "He's gone away for some time, perhaps for five years."

"Better make it ten," said Nana, giving Posy a quick kiss. "That'll give us a chance."

About four months later a box arrived at the house in the Cromwell Road, addressed to "The Little Fossils." Inside were three necklaces: a turquoise one with "Pauline" on it; a tiny string of seed pearls marked "Petrova," and a row of coral for Posy.

"Well," said Nana, fastening the necklaces round the children's necks. "I expect that's the last we shall hear of him for some time."

And she was quite right.

II

The Boarders

*

PAULINE, PETROVA AND POSY had a very ordinary
nursery life. Not a great many toys, because they had
no relations to give them any. There was a good deal
of passing down of clothes, because there was not a
great amount of money and no one knew when Gum
would be back to provide any more.

"It does seem mean, Nana," Sylvia said. "Posy
never gets any new clothes at all, and Petrova hardly
any, while Pauline has them all the time."

"Ah, well"—Nana looked proudly at Pauline—
"so it is in a good many nurseries, and I must say if
anyone is going to have them it's a good thing it's her.
Pauline does pay for dressing."

So Pauline did. By the time she was four she was
really lovely. A mass of almost white curls, huge blue
eyes, and the sort of pink-and-white look seen in the
best babies. Sylvia secretly admired Petrova more. She
thought she looked interesting. She was too pale and
too thin, but she had deep-set brown eyes, and hair the
color of a jay's wing. Posy, at two, suddenly surprised

everybody by becoming red-headed. Up till then she had very little hair, and that mostly mouse-colored; but one morning a little red showed, and then after a week or two she was quite decidedly ginger.

"I never have cared for red hair," Nana said fondly, twisting a strand of Posy's round her finger. "Never could fancy it since I got scratched by a ginger cat as a child. But nicely kept it can be striking."

As soon as the children could talk there was trouble about a name for them to call Sylvia by. Nana refused to allow her Christian name to be used.

"It's not suitable, Miss. They can say 'Miss Brown' or if you are willing, 'Aunty' or 'Cousin Sylvia,' but just 'Sylvia' is rude and I'm not having it in my nursery."

"But Nana," Sylvia argued, "I do hate 'Aunt' and 'Cousin,' and it isn't as if I was one."

"What are you?" Pauline asked. "If you're not a cousin nor nuffin'?"

"A guardian, darling." Sylvia pulled her on to her knee. "What would you like to call me?"

"Garnian." Pauline spoke the word with care. "Garnian."

"That's very nice, Pauline." Nana approved. "You shall all call Miss Brown Guardian, and very suitable too."

Of course she never was called Guardian, as it was too long and severe, but they compromised on Garnie, which satisfied everybody.

Pauline had a birthday in December, and when she was just going to be six, Nana came to Sylvia one night when the three children were in bed.

"It's time Pauline had education, and it wouldn't hurt Petrova either—she's sharp as a cartload of monkeys; do her good to have something to think about. What with my nurseries, and Posy still no more than a baby, I've no time to be setting sums and that. Now, will you teach them, Miss, or shall they go to school?"

Sylvia looked horrified.

"Me teach them? Goodness! I couldn't. I was always a perfect fool at arithmetic. We'll send them to school."

So Pauline and Petrova were sent to the junior house of a day school quite near their home. It was called Cromwell House, and they had jade-green coats, tunics and berets; the tunics and berets had C.H. embroidered on them. Both the children were frightfully proud of themselves.

"You wouldn't think, Garnie," Petrova said when she came to show herself off in her school outfit, "that here is a child who won't be five till August."

"You only look a baby." Pauline put her nose in

the air. "Now, anybody can see I was six last month."

One morning at school it was discovered that the children had no real surname. Sylvia came to fetch them at twelve, and they shot out of the door and clustered about her.

"Garnie, what is my real, honest surname?" Pauline asked. "They said it was Brown, but I told them it wasn't, because Nana always says that you are no relation."

Sylvia took each of them by the hand.

"But, darlings, I entered you both as Brown. What other name can I give you?"

"It's not our real name," Pauline objected.

Petrova gave a tug at her hand to attract attention.

"Garnie, on my necklace what Gum sent, he called us Fossil."

"So he did." Pauline nodded emphatically. "Fossil is a lovely name and our very own. I'm Pauline Fossil." She leaned across to Petrova, "And you're Petrova Fossil. Oh——" She suddenly stood still.

"What is it?" Sylvia asked.

Pauline looked at Petrova.

"We don't want Posy to be a Fossil, do we?"

"No," said Petrova decidedly.

"But why not?" Sylvia laughed. "You can be

Fossil if you like, but I think you may as well all have the same name."

"Well, me and Pauline are at school," Petrova explained, "and that Posy is only a child."

"We mightn't care to share a name with her when she's older, you see," Pauline added.

"I don't see," Sylvia said decidedly. "Posy is a darling. However, run up to the nursery and see what she and Nana have to say."

She opened the front door.

Posy was toddling about the nursery, pushing a wooden horse. Pauline and Petrova caught hold of her.

"Posy, do you want to be called Fossil?"

"Ess," said Posy, who had no idea what they were talking about.

"Want to call her what?" asked Nana.

The children explained. It took her quite a time to grasp the discussion as they both talked at once.

"Fossil"—she pursed up her lips—"well, it's not a name I ever heard before, not for children. It's what the Professor called all those dirty stones he brought home."

"But he did call us it too." Pauline skipped about excitedly.

"So he did." Nana went on with her darning. "It's a funny name, but it's as good as another."

Petrova leaned up against her knee.

"We were asking Posy if she wanted it too. She said yes; but, then, she's so silly she says yes to everything."

Nana looked up, surprised.

"If you're a Fossil, so's Posy. I'm not having a whole lot of surnames in my nursery. You're all three P. Fossil; one lot of marking tapes all through."

Posy was to be six in September. Nana came to Sylvia in August.

"Posy'll be six next month. It's dull for her stuck in the nursery alone. I thought maybe she should start at Cromwell House next term."

Sylvia walked to the window. Nana noticed disapprovingly that she had got very thin lately, and that her hair was turning gray.

"Nana." Sylvia swung the blind-cord to and fro. "Do you realize the Professor has been gone almost six years?"

Nana smoothed her apron.

"Must have been; he went just when Posy came to us."

"Before he left he arranged with the bank about money for us all. Enough for five years."

Nana looked startled.

"And it's finished?"

"Almost. Of course, I have tried to save, as you never can be sure of the Professor."

Nana pursed her lips in a disapproving way, but all she said was,

"No, indeed, Miss."

"So the thing is," Sylvia went on, "I can't send Posy to school. As a matter of fact, I've got to take the others away, and even then. . . ."

Nana never could remember that though she had been Sylvia's nurse, her child was now a grown-up woman, and the sound of the sort of crack in the voice that people get when they are miserable brought all her nurse instincts to the top.

"There, there, dear," she said comfortingly. "Don't you fuss, there's a way round everything if you look for it."

Sylvia gave a miserable smile.

"I hope you are right; but there's a way round a good many things wanted in this house. First there's the cost of looking after a house when there isn't any money. There's you, and the other servants, and we all eat a lot."

Nana thought a moment, then her face lit up.

"How about boarders? Such a lot of empty rooms we have. Why don't we take some nice people in?"

"Boarders!" Sylvia looked startled. "I don't think the Professor would like them."

"What the eye doesn't see, the heart doesn't grieve after. When I take Posy out tomorrow I'll step into Harrods and put an advertisement in the paper."

"Oh, but Nana, the house will want a lot of alterations before we can take in anybody."

"Nothing that a bit of shopping and a carpenter can't do in a week or two. We shan't get answers all that quick. What I say is, if you've got to do a thing, don't let the grass grow."

"Then there's the children's education. What about that?"

Nana patted the cushions straight on the sofa.

"I remember Miss Edwards that taught you," she said casually, "telling me you were very good at your books."

"Oh, Nana!" Sylvia was horrified. "You don't think I ought to teach them. I never could do arithmetic."

"There's other learning without sums."

Sylvia shook her head.

"Reading, writing and arithmetic, you can't do proper lessons without those."

"It won't be for long," Nana urged. "The Professor will be back soon. I reckon you'd know enough to teach them just till he comes."

"I might Pauline, but never Petrova! She's terribly good at figures."

"When I'm in Harrods with Posy in the morning, I'll get you a book on figures. I've seen the kind that had sums set one end, and answers the other. You don't need to know anything to write those down." She got up. "Well, I'll be along to my bed, if you'll excuse me. We've a big day in front of us tomorrow getting set for the boarders and all."

The three children found it fun helping to change the rooms round. Nana was busy all day long making chair-covers and curtains, and had not much time for them, so sometimes they went with Sylvia to buy furniture and choose eiderdowns, sometimes they helped in the kitchen, and sometimes, when nobody noticed, they assisted the decorators who were distempering the boarders' walls. It was, in fact, almost like a holiday; it is so nice doing things you do not usually do.

One afternoon when they were all three in the kitchen the front-door bell rang. Cook was teaching Pauline to make buns, Clara, the housemaid, was ironing, Posy was making animals out of pastry, and Petrova was sitting on the table in the window reading

a book about Citröen cars which had come as an
advertisement.

"Drat that bell!" said Clara. "How am I going to
get these hung tomorrow in a boarder's room if that
bell keeps ringing?"

"It hasn't before," Pauline pointed out reasonably.
"We've been down here simply hours, and it hasn't
rung once."

The bell rang again.

"Ought to be answered." Cook spoke firmly, partly
because her word was law in the kitchen, and partly
because whoever answered it, it would not be her. She
looked round, but everybody seemed busy; then her
eye fell on Petrova. Reading was not an occupation.
It came in her view under the heading of "Satan
finds. . . ."

"Petrova dear," she said, "we're all busy; you run
up and see who it is." When Petrova had gone she
excused herself to Clara. "It isn't what Nana or Miss
Brown would hold with, but with us so busy, I must
break a rule or two. Most likely it's only somebody
begging."

Petrova ran up the stairs, and opened the front door
with some difficulty, because the thing you turned was
stiff. Outside were a gentleman and lady. They smiled
at Petrova, but she forgot all her manners and failed to

smile back; instead she stared past them into the road, where stood the very Citröen car whose picture she had been looking at in the kitchen. She turned to the man.

"Is that yours?"

"Yes. I got it last week."

"Oh!" Petrova looked longingly at the bonnet; she would have liked a look at the inside. The man, who was very fond of insides of cars himself, sensed her interest.

"Nice cars," he said. "Come and have a look."

Petrova came, and together they examined it, and she asked questions and he explained. At last the lady patted his shoulder.

"John, dear, we didn't come here to show off the car, but to look at rooms."

Petrova raised her face, her eyes sparkling with pleasure.

"How lovely! When Garnie said we would have to take boarders I never did think of a car coming to live here."

The man laughed.

"It's us that will live here if we take the rooms, not the car, you know. It isn't house-trained. Look, here is my card; will you take us to your mother and say we want to see the rooms?"

Petrova spelled out the words on the card.

"John Simpson. Kuala Lumpur. Malay."

"Are you Mrs. Simpson?" she asked the lady.

"Yes."

"Did you come all the way from Malay too?"

"Yes."

"A long way," Petrova said politely. "Long enough away to be in a Geography lesson."

Mrs. Simpson stooped and put her arm round her.

"Could you take that card to your mother and ask if we could see the rooms?"

"I haven't got a mother," Petrova explained. "There's Garnie, and there's Nana. Which would you rather have?"

"Is Garnie the one who owns the house?" Mrs. Simpson asked.

Petrova considered the question.

"I don't think exactly, I think truly it belongs to Gum; but he's been away on a boat for years, an' years, an' years—ever since he brought Posy. Garnie sort of has the house because he's away. She's his great-niece, you see."

"Well, could we see Garnie?"

Mrs. Simpson moved towards the front door.

Petrova put on her best manners.

"Course. Please come in."

When she had safely handed the Simpsons to Sylvia she went back to the kitchen.

"What was it?" Clara asked. "You've been a time. What've you been doing?"

"Imagine"—Petrova's face was quite pink with pleasure—"it was a Citröen car, and it's coming here as a boarder."

"A car!" Clara laid down her iron. "Do you mean to say we're starting a garage? If so, what are these curtains for?"

"There were two people with it," Petrova explained. "Mr. and Mrs. Simpson; they come from Malay."

Pauline turned to Cook.

"That's the bit next to India, where india-rubbers come out of trees."

"And motor tires," Petrova reminded her.

"Never you two mind about Malay," Cook said firmly, "quite enough to be able to buy a bit of india-rubber, no need asking where it comes from. Is this Mr. and Mrs. Simpson taking the rooms, Petrova?"

Petrova looked surprised.

"That's what they've come for. They wouldn't come if they didn't want them, would they?"

"Ah!" Clara put her iron to her face to feel how hot it was. "There's a lot come to look at rooms, but do they take them?"

"Don't they never take them?" Posy inquired.

"One in a million," said Cook. "That's my experience."

The Simpsons seemed to be the one in a million; they said they would be on leave for six months, or perhaps longer, and they would move into Cromwell Road the next Monday. Garnie told Petrova that she considered she had done the letting, and she would take her to the motor show as a reward.

The next tenant was a Miss Theo Dane. She was an instructress of dancing at "The Children's Academy of Dancing and Stage Training." She was little and pretty, and wanted a room on the ground floor so that she would not disturb anybody when she was practicing. The children stared at her over the stairs when she moved in.

"I thought she would wear shoes like the ones your mother left you," Pauline whispered to Posy.

Posy thought of the tiny pale pink satin ballet shoes upstairs.

"Not when it's raining," she suggested.

"Look!" Petrova, who was in the middle, dug an elbow into each of them. "What's that red box?"

She spoke louder than she knew. Theo Dane looked up and smiled.

"It's a big phonograph. Perhaps you'll come down

and hear it when I've arranged my things. Will you?"

Pauline skipped down the stairs.

"Can we come after tea?"

"That'll be very nice."

Petrova followed Pauline.

"All of us, or just Pauline?"

"All of you."

They went, and found the gramophone very nice indeed. Theo let Pauline and Petrova wind it and change the records. Posy began to dance as soon as the music started; the other two were a bit shocked.

"You mustn't mind. She doesn't mean to show off —it's because she's little."

"It's not showing off," said Theo, who was watching Posy with interest. "Why don't we all dance? It's the right thing to do to music."

It did seem to be, for she put on a record which had the most dancing effect on the feet, even on Petrova's, which were the least dancing feet in the family.

When Nana came to fetch Posy to bed, she found a most hot, disheveled party.

"Well, you have been having a time." She smoothed Posy's hair. "Thank Miss Dane nicely, Posy, and say good night."

Theo kissed Posy. She looked anxiously at Nana.

"I hope we haven't made too much noise."

"There was plenty," Nana said. "But it hasn't done any harm. We let the other two rooms while you were at it."

The three children threw themselves at her.

"Who, Nana? Did they look nice?"

"Have they got cars?"

"Have they got a phonograph?"

"One at a time," Nana said firmly. "They are both doctors—lady doctors."

"Lady doctors!" Pauline made a face remembering various bottles of medicine that she had not cared for. "I don't think we want those in the house. Nobody's ill."

"These aren't the sort that come when you're ill," Nana explained. "Doctors for learning, they are. They coach."

Posy looked interested.

"Like the picture of John Gilpin? 'My sister, and my sister's child.' That one?"

Nana shook her head.

"No. Miss Brown says their sort of coaching is teaching. Come on, Posy."

Pauline and Petrova went to the drawing-room, where Sylvia always read to them for a bit before they went to bed. They were reading a book called *The Secret Garden* which had belonged to Sylvia when she was a child. Neither Pauline nor Petrova could sit quietly while they were being read to, however interesting the book, without something to do. Pauline had sewing, and embroidered very well for somebody not yet ten. Petrova was very stupid with her needle, but very neat with her fingers; she was working at a model made in Meccano. It was a difficult model of an aeroplane, meant for much older children to make. Sylvia opened the book.

"Garnie," said Pauline, "do you think you are going to like having boarders?"

"I shan't." Petrova screwed in a tiny nut. "Houses is meant for families, not for strangers."

Pauline wriggled excitedly on her chair.

"I shall like Miss Dane. Oh, Garnie, she has such a lovely phonograph!"

"I shall like Mr. and Mrs. Simpson best, because of their car."

Pauline nodded at Sylvia.

"You'll have to like the poor doctors, then; it's mean they shouldn't be liked by anybody."

"I shall like all the boarders," Sylvia said firmly, "because they are going to pay enough money to help me to bring you up properly." She opened the book. "Do you remember where we had got to last time?"

III

The Fossil Family Makes a Vow

*

PAULINE had a cold, and she was left at home when Nana took Petrova and Posy for their walk. She was in that state of having a cold when nothing is very nice to do. Sylvia had got her a piece of linen and some colored thread, and she could have started on the dressing-table cover she was going to give Nana for her birthday. Cook had invited her to come to the kitchen and make toffee. Clara brought in a page of transfers, and suggested she stick them on a book to "Give to a poor child in a hospital." Nana, who remembered how one felt with colds, gave her some brass polish and the sets of brass out of the dolls' house.

"I expect those to shine when we get in," she said firmly. "Much better to have something to do. No good sitting around thinking how miserable you feel."

The last being an order, and as Nana expected things done when she said they were to be, Pauline finished them first. She found them quite fun to do, but she worked at them so hard that in half an hour they could not shine more than they did. Pauline put

them back in the dolls' house, and thought for a moment of rearranging the drawing-room, but decided it
would not be any fun without the others. She looked
at the clock and wished it was tea-time, but it was only
three. She took out the linen, and even threaded a bit of
thread; but somehow she did not feel "sewish," so she
put it back in her drawer. She decided as there was not
anything else to do she had better go and make the
toffee; but she felt hot, and not very much like eating
toffee, and what is the fun of making toffee unless you
want to eat it. She sat down on the landing of the
second floor and sniffed and thought how beastly colds
were. At that moment the door behind her opened and
a head popped out. It had a shawl around it, and for a
moment Pauline was not sure who it was. Then she
recognized that it was one of the lady doctors—the one
whose surname was Jakes. Doctor Jakes looked at Pauline.

"My dear child, what are you doing there by yourself?"

"I'b god a coad," Pauline explained stuffily, for she
had come down without her handkerchief. "And the
others hab god out withoud me, and I habbent god
edythig to do."

Doctor Jakes laughed.

"You sound as though you *have* got a cold. So have

I, as a matter of fact. Come in. I've got a lovely fire, and I'll lend you a large silk handkerchief, and I'll give you some ginger drink which is doing me good."

Pauline came in at once. She liked the sound of the whole of the invitation. Besides, she had not seen the inside of the two doctors' rooms since they had been boarders' rooms instead of homes for Gum's fossils. As a matter of fact, this one had changed so she felt it was a new room altogether. It had owned a rather shabby wall-paper; but when the boarder idea started it was distempered a sort of pale primrose all over. But the primrose hardly showed now, for the whole walls were covered with books.

"My goodness!" said Pauline, walking round and blowing her nose on the scarlet silk handkerchief Doctor Jakes provided. "You must read an awful lot. We have a big book-shelf in the nursery, but that's for all of us and Nana. Fancy all these just for you!"

Doctor Jakes came over to the shelves.

"Literature is my subject."

"Is it? Is that what you're a doctor of?"

"More or less. But apart from that, books are very ornamental things to have about."

Pauline looked at the shelves. These books certainly were grand-looking—all smooth shiny covers, and lots of gold on them.

"Ours aren't very," she said frankly. "Yours are more all one size. We have things next to each other like *Peter Rabbit* and *Just So Stories,* and they don't match very well."

"No, but very good reading."

Pauline came to the fire. It was a lovely fire; she stood looking at the logs on it.

"Do you think *Peter Rabbit* good reading? I would have thought a person who taught literature was too grand for it."

"Not a bit—very old friend of mine."

Pauline looked at the shawl.

"Why do you wear that round your head?"

"Because I had earache with my cold. Have you got earache with yours?"

"No. Just my nose."

Pauline remembered the ginger drink, and looked round for it. Doctor Jakes remembered it at the same time. She put on the kettle.

"Sit down. This drink is made with boiling water, and takes quite a time. Have you a holiday from school because of your cold?"

Pauline explained that they did not go to Cromwell House any more, and why.

"You see," she said, "Gum said he'd be back in five years, and he isn't."

"And who exactly is Gum?"

Doctor Jakes poured things out of various bottles into two glasses.

Pauline hugged her knees.

"Well, he's called Gum because he's Garnie's Great-Uncle Matthew. He isn't really a great uncle of ours, because we haven't any relations. I was rescued off a ship, Petrova is an orphan from Russia, and Posy's father is dead, and her mother couldn't afford to have her, so we've made ourselves into sisters. We've called ourselves Fossil because that's what Gum called us. He brought us back instead of them, you see."

"I see. Rather exciting choosing your own name and your own relations."

"Yes." Pauline saw that the kettle was nearly boiling and looked hopefully at the glasses. "We almost didn't choose Posy to be a Fossil. She was little and stupid then, but she's all right now."

Doctor Jakes got up and took the kettle off the fire and poured the water on the mixture in the glasses. At once there was the most lovely hot sweet smell. Pauline sniffed.

"That smells good."

Doctor Jakes put the tumblers into silver frames with handles, and passed one to Pauline.

"I do envy you. I should think it an adventure to

have a name like that, and sisters by accident. The three of you might make the name of Fossil really important, really worth while, and if you do, it's all your own. Now, if I make Jakes really worth while, people will say I take after my grandfather or something.''

Pauline sipped her drink. It was very hot, but simply heavenly—the sort of drink certain to make a cold feel better. She looked across at Doctor Jakes over the rim of the glass, her eyes shining.

''Do you suppose Petrova and Posy and I could make Fossil an important sort of name?''

''Of course. Making your name worth while is a very nice thing to do; it means you must have given distinguished service to your country in some way.''

Pauline gave another gulp at her drink. She frowned thoughtfully.

''I don't think we do the things that make names important. I sew, and Petrova's awfully good at works of things—she can mend clocks and she knows heaps about aeroplanes and motor-cars. Posy doesn't do much yet.''

''There's time. You probably won't develop a talent till you are fourteen or fifteen. Are you good at lessons?''

''Well, we were. Petrova was very good at sums, and I said poetry the best in the class; but it's different now we learn with Garnie. You know, she has to teach Posy too, and she has to do the baby things, like learning her letters, and it takes a lot of time. Petrova does sums well still, but Garnie just puts R. R. R.; she never teaches her a new one. I say poetry sometimes, but not very often now."

"What sort of poetry do you like?"

"All sorts. We learnt 'Oh to be in England' and 'The Ancient Mariner,' and I had just started 'Hiawatha.' "

"Do you ever learn any Shakespeare?"

"No. I should have started 'As You Like It' the next term if I had stayed at Cromwell House."

"You should learn him. He wrote a few good parts for children. If you are fond of reciting, that's the stuff to work at." She went over to her shelves and picked out a book, and opened it. "Listen."

She read the scene in "King John" between Prince Arthur and Hubert. Pauline did not understand it all, but Doctor Jakes was one of those people who really can read out loud. She forgot to drink her ginger, and instead, listened so hard that at last Doctor Jakes vanished, and in her place she saw a cowering little boy pleading for his eyes.

"There." Doctor Jakes closed the book. "Learn

that. Learn to play Prince Arthur so that we cringe at the hot irons just as he does, and then you can talk about reciting." She got another book, found the place and passed it to Pauline. "You read me that."

It was Puck's speech which begins "Fairy, thou speak'st aright." Pauline had never seen it before, and she halted over some of the words, but she got a remarkable amount of the feeling of Puck into it. When she had finished, Doctor Jakes nodded at her in a pleased way.

"Good! We'll read some more one day. I'll make a Shakespearean of you."

Pauline heard the front door slam and got up.

"There's the others, I must go. Thank you very much for the ginger drink."

"Good-bye." Doctor Jakes did not look up; she was studying "The Midsummer Night's Dream." "Don't forget, it's fun having a name with no background. Tell the other Fossils."

After tea Pauline told Petrova and Posy what Doctor Jakes had said. Petrova was most impressed.

"Do you think she meant we could make it a name in history books?"

Pauline was not sure.

"She didn't exactly say history books, but I think

that's what she meant. She said making your name worth while means you must have given distinguished service to your country."

Petrova's eyes shone.

"How lovely if we could! Fancy people learning about us as lessons! Let's make a vow to make Fossil a name like that."

Pauline looked serious.

"A real vow, do you mean, like at christenings?"

"Yes." Petrova hopped she was so excited. "Like 'promise and vow three things. . . .' "

"What about her?" Pauline pointed at Posy, who, not understanding the conversation, was dressing her Teddy bear.

"Posy"—Petrova knelt down beside her—"do you know what making a vow is?"

"No." Posy held out a little pair of blue trousers. "These don't fit Teddy any more."

Pauline took Teddy and his clothes from her.

"You must listen, Posy," she said in a very grown-up voice. "This is important. A vow is a promise; it's a thing when you've made it you've got to do it. Do you understand?"

"Yes." Posy held out her hand. "Give me Teddy."

"No." Petrova took her hand. "Not till we've finished the vowing." She turned to Pauline. "You say it, and Posy and I will hold up our hands and say 'We vow.' "

Pauline put both her feet together and folded her hands.

"We three Fossils," she said in a church voice, "vow to try and put our name in history books because it's our very own and nobody can say it's because of our grandfathers."

She made a face at Petrova, who hurriedly held up her right arm, and grabbed Posy's and held it up, too.

"We vow." She said this so low down in her inside that it sounded terribly impressive, then she whispered to Posy "Go on, say 'We vow.' "

"We vow."

Posy tried to say it in the same deep voice as Petrova, but she did it wrong, and it sounded rather like a cat meowing. This made them all laugh, and the big vowing, instead of ending seriously, found them laughing so much that they fell on the floor, and their tummies ached.

Pauline was the first to recover.

"Oh, we oughtn't to have laughed!" She wiped her eyes. "But, Posy, you did sound silly!" She gave another gurgle. "Shall we make this same vow over again on each of our birthdays?"

"Let's," agreed Petrova. "It'll make our birthdays so important."

"We vow," Posy said in exactly the same me-ow.

This time they could not stop laughing, and they were still giggling when it was time to go down to be read to by Sylvia.

Boarders had not settled Sylvia's troubles. It was quite obvious that children with no certain future ought to be brought up with the kind of education that meant they could earn their own living later on. The kind of education that she was able to give them could not, as far as she could see, fit them for anything. She kept this worry to herself, but it was such a bad one it kept her awake at nights.

Then one day she had three visitors. The first two came after lunch. She had just sat down to read the paper when there was a knock on her door. She was feeling very tired, for planning food for a lot of boarders as well as giving three children lessons is tiring. She was not in the mood to see anybody; but if you take in boarders you have to put up with seeing them when you do not want to, so she said "Come in" as politely as she could. It was the two doctors—Doctor Jakes and Doctor Smith. Doctor Jakes wasted no time.

"My dear," she said, sitting down in an armchair

facing Sylvia. "I doubt if you are qualified to teach those children."

Sylvia flushed.

"I'm not," she agreed humbly.

"That's what we thought." Doctor Smith drew up a small chair and sat down next to Doctor Jakes. "But, you see, we are."

"Yes." Sylvia fiddled with her fingers. "I know you are, but I can't pay anybody who is."

"We thought that too." Doctor Smith looked at Doctor Jakes. "You tell her."

Doctor Jakes cleared her throat.

"We should like to teach them. For nothing."

"For nothing! Why?" asked Sylvia.

"Why not?" said Doctor Smith.

"But they're not your children," Sylvia protested.

"Nor yours," Doctor Jakes suggested.

"Mine by adoption," Sylvia said firmly.

"Mayn't we help?" Doctor Jakes leaned forward. "We thought we should like to retire. It would give us time for research, but we find we miss our teaching. Pauline has a beautiful ear for verse-speaking, and I shall enjoy training her."

"Mathematics is my subject," Doctor Smith explained. "I hear Petrova is fond of mathematics."

Sylvia looked at Doctor Smith as though she were an angel.

"You teach arithmetic?" Her voice was awed. "You are offering to teach the children?"

"That's right." Both the doctors spoke at once.

"I think Heaven must have sent you to this house. I accept your offer more gratefully than I can say." Sylvia turned to Doctor Smith. "Would you mind starting tomorrow? I simply can't give another arithmetic lesson."

The two doctors got up.

"Yes, tomorrow," Doctor Jakes agreed. "All-round education, specializing in mathematics and literature. The children to be prepared to take the school certificate and matriculation."

That night after dinner Sylvia had her third visitor. It was Theo Dane. She knocked, and at the same time popped her head round the drawing-room door.

"May I come in? I want a word with you." She did not wait for permission, but came in, and sat down on the floor at Sylvia's feet. "You know I teach dancing at The Children's Academy of Dancing and Stage Training?"

"Yes." Sylvia went on stitching at the curtains she was hemming.

"The head is Madame Fidolia. You remember she was a big dancer in the years before the war?"

Sylvia did not really remember the name, but it seemed rude to say so, so she gave a sort of half cough, half yes.

"Well," Theo went on, "I spoke to her today about your three. She'll have them."

"Have them?" Sylvia looked puzzled. "How do you mean?"

"Teach them. Take them as pupils."

"But I couldn't pay the fees."

"She'll take them free. I told her about them, and what a time you were having, and she'll train them. She'll hope to make something out of them later when they're working."

"Working! What at?"

"On the stage. It's a stage school."

Sylvia's mouth opened.

"But I don't want the children to go on the stage."

"Why not?" Theo half got up in her earnestness. "Posy has the makings of a real dancer. I've tried her out to my phonograph. Pauline is lovely to look at, and she has a good sense of rhythm."

"Do you mean they should earn money at it?"

"Of course. They have no parents or relations; it's a good thing for them to have a career."

"But I'm instead of parents and relations."

"But suppose you were run over by a bus. Wouldn't it be a good thing if they were trained to help support themselves?"

"But there's my Great-Uncle Matthew. They are really his wards."

"Where is he?"

"On a voyage," Sylvia explained, and then added, "He's been on it for some years."

"Quite," agreed Theo, obviously considering Gum as somebody so unlikely to appear as to matter no more than a ghost. "Well, what do you say? Isn't it a good idea?"

Sylvia looked worried.

"I don't think Nana would approve; and then there are the doctors upstairs. They are going to educate them. What'll they say?"

"That's easy," said Theo. "Let's have them all down and ask them."

Nana and the two doctors came down and heard Theo's suggestion. Then Sylvia said:

"I have told her that I don't think we can consider it."

"Why not?" asked Nana.

"Oh, Nana"—Sylvia was flushed—"I thought you'd be certain to agree with me."

"And for why?" Nana smoothed a crease out of her apron. "Posy we may say is bound to dance anyway, coming to us with her dancing slippers and all. It might be just the right thing for Pauline too——never any good at her books, only fond of that reciting."

"How about Petrova?" said Sylvia.

"Well, she won't be good at it to my way of thinking, but it might be just the thing for her——turn her more like a little lady; always messing about with the works of clocks and that just like a boy; never plays with dolls, and takes no more interest in her clothes than a scarecrow."

"What do you think?" Sylvia turned to the two doctors.

Doctor Jakes looked at Doctor Smith and they nodded at each other. Then Doctor Jakes cleared her throat.

"It's a great responsibility, my dear, for you to undertake, but we do feel Miss Dane's suggestion is good. It may be that you may find later that dancing is not the career for all of them, but the training will have done them good, and you will at least have taken a step towards trying to make them self-supporting."

Sylvia looked round at them all; she felt she must take their advice, but she was worried.

"They are such little children," she exclaimed.

Nana got up.

"Little children grow up. I suppose that Anna Pavlova was a little child once. I'll be going back to my nurseries, if you'll excuse me, Miss Sylvia dear. Good night."

IV

Madame Fidolia and the Dancing Class

*

THE CHILDREN'S ACADEMY OF DANCING AND STAGE TRAINING was in Bloomsbury. It was three large houses joined inside by passages. Across the front was written in large gold letters: "Children's Acad" on the first house, "emy of Dancing an" on the second, and "d Stage Training" on the third. Theo had arranged that Nana and Sylvia should take the children round to see the place and to meet Madame Fidolia on a Wednesday afternoon, and that they should start their classes on the following Monday. Since it was a very important occasion, Mr. Simpson said he would drive them all to the Academy in his car. The afternoon started badly. Pauline wanted to wear a party frock, which she said was the right thing for a dancing class; Nana, after discussion with Theo, had ironed and washed their blue-linen smocks and knickers.

"I want to wear our muslins," said Pauline. "At Cromwell House girls who learned dancing wore best frocks."

"Only for ballroom dancing," Petrova argued.

"They wore silk tunics for everything else; we haven't got those."

Nana was firm.

"It's not a matter of what you've got or haven't got; you're putting on the smocks and knickers I've laid on your beds, so get on with changing while I dress Posy."

"Why can't we wear our muslins?" Pauline growled.

"Because for the exercises and that they're going to see you do Miss Dane said plain cotton frocks and knickers. When you start on Monday you're having rompers, two each, black-patent ankle-strap shoes, and white tarlatan dresses, two each, with white sandal shoes, and white knickers, two pairs, all frills; so don't worry me, because I'm going to have worries enough getting all that lot made by Monday."

Petrova pulled off her pink check frock and knickers, and got into the clean ones.

"What do we want all those for?"

Nana sighed.

"Ask me, dear! What we've got would do quite well for dancing in, I should say; but there's a printed list come, and there's all that on it, not to mention two rough face-towels for each child, clearly marked, and two special overalls to be bought through the school.

Now you know. Come here, Pauline, and let me see to your hair."

Petrova hurried through her dressing and ran downstairs. She found Mr. Simpson sitting in his car.

"Hullo!" he called. "Come beside me." She scrambled in. He looked down at her and smiled. "So they are going to train you as a dancer, are they?"

"Yes." Petrova sighed. "And I don't want to be one."

"Why? Might be fun."

"Not for me; I'm not any good. At Cromwell House we did dancing games once a week, and I was the worst in the class. Pauline was the best, though."

"How about Posy?"

"Her mother was a dancer, she became a Fossil bringing ballet shoes with her, so I expect she'll be all right." She fiddled with the gear lever. "Do you suppose if you train to be a dancer and to act when you are eight like me, that you can be something else when you grow up?"

"Of course." He laughed. "Eight isn't very old. You've at least another ten years before you'll need to worry."

"Oh, no." Petrova shook her head. "Nana says that Miss Dane says that we can start to earn money when we are twelve. I shall be twelve in four years. So

if I begin earning then, I shall have been doing it for"
—she counted on her fingers—"five years by the time
I'm quite grown-up."

"Meaning you'd be quite grown-up at seventeen?"

"Yes. Well, would you think then I could be something else?"

"Of course. What do you want to be?"

"I don't know quite. Something to do with driving
cars. Can girls be chauffeurs?"

"Lots are."

She looked pleased.

"Then I think I'll be that."

When they arrived at the Academy and rang the
bell they were shown into a waiting-room. They had
to wait in it quite a long time; but the children did not
mind because of the pictures on the walls. These were
photographs of the pupils of the school. Some were
large ones of just one child. These were rather alike—
the child wearing a ballet frock and standing on her
toes. These were signed: "To dear Madame Fidolia
from Little Doris," or "Babsy," or "Baby Cora," or
names like that. The children were most impressed by
the way the children in the photographs stood on their
points, but shocked at the signatures, considering them
all too old to have names like "Little" or "Babsy" or
"Baby."

They played a game giving marks for the hand-writings; in the end a child signing herself "Tiny" won. The photographs they liked better were the groups. These were of pantomimes, and though there were lots of Academy pupils in them, the children were not interested. What they liked were the other characters.

"Look," said Posy, climbing on a seat to see better. "That's 'The Three Bears'."

"It's not." Pauline got up and joined her. "It says it's 'Puss in Boots'."

Petrova came over to study the picture.

"I think it must have been called wrong. It is 'The Three Bears.' What are those?"

Pauline put her head on one side hoping to see better.

"More like three cats, I think."

"But there isn't three cats in 'Puss in Boots'," Posy objected. "There's only one cat."

Petrova suddenly gave an exclamation.

"Look. Those three cats aren't grown-up people; they are much smaller than that lady in tights." She turned to Sylvia. "Would you suppose when I'm twelve and can earn money I could be a cat? I wouldn't mind that."

"No." Pauline jumped off the bench. "I'd love to

be a cat, or a dog. A Pekinese would be nice to be—
such a furry coat."

"It's a monkey you'll be in a minute climbing about
messing yourself up," Nana interrupted. "Come and
sit down like little ladies."

Posy sat next to Sylvia.

"I'd rather be dressed like one of those little girls,"
she said thoughtfully. "I'd like to wear flowers in my
hair."

Pauline and Petrova looked at each other.

"Would you think," said Pauline, "that there could
be so vain a child?" She turned to Posy. "And I suppose you'd like to be called 'Baby Posy'?"

"I wouldn't mind." Posy swung her legs happily.
"I'd like to look like one of those children."

Petrova turned toward her, and spoke in a very
shocked voice.

"You wouldn't really like to look like one of those
dressed-up misses? You wouldn't, Posy. You'd really
much rather be a cat."

"No." Posy lolled against Sylvia. "I'd like to wear
flowers in my hair. Cats don't."

"Very nice, too," said Nana. "Cats, indeed; it's
the Zoo you two ought to train at, not a dancing
school."

Pauline and Petrova both started to argue when they

were interrupted. The door opened, and Madame Fidolia came in. Madame Fidolia had been a great dancer many years before; she had started training at the age of seven in the Russian Imperial Ballet School. She had made a big name for herself before the War, not only in Russia, but all over the world. When the revolution came she had to leave her country, for she had been a favorite with the Czar and Czarina, and so not popular with Red Russia. She made London her new home, and for some years danced there, as well as in most of the European capitals and America. Then one morning she had waked up and decided she was too old to dance any more. At the same time she realized she was too energetic a person to lead a lazy life, so she started her academy.

Madame Fidolia had thought, when she opened it, that she would run it as the Old Imperial Ballet School had been run. She soon found that was impossible, as it would cost far more money than pupils would pay. She found, too, that there were very few children who came to her who had real talent. She had discovered none of whom she had made a first-class ballerina. So she gave up trying to do the impossible, and ran an ordinary stage school where the children learned all kinds of dancing, and actors came to teach them the art of acting. There was only one class through which they did not all pass, and that was Madame Fidolia's own. She watched every pupil who came through the school with care for about three to six months and then perhaps one day she would say: "My child, you will come to my classes next term." Going to Madame Fidolia's classes was the highest honor of the Academy.

The children thought her very odd-looking. She had come straight from teaching. She had black hair parted in the middle and drawn down tight into a small bun on her neck. She had on a long practice dress of white tarlatan, and pink tights, and pink ballet shoes. Round her shoulders she had a cerise silk shawl. She stood in the doorway.

"Miss Brown?" She had a very pretty, broken accent.

Sylvia got up.

"I'm Miss Brown." They shook hands. Madame looked at the children.

"My pupils?"

"Yes. This is Pauline."

Pauline smiled shyly and held out her hand, but Madame shook her head.

"No. All my children when they see me night and morning, and before and after a class, or any time when we meet say, 'Madame' and curtsy. So!" She swept a lovely curtsy down to the floor.

Pauline turned scarlet, but she managed somehow, though it was more a bob than a curtsy, and only "am" of "Madame" could be heard.

"And this is Petrova."

Petrova started her curtsy, but Madame came across to her. She took her face between her hands.

"Are you Russian?"

"Yes."

"You speak Russian?" Madame's tone was full of hope.

"No." Petrova looked anxiously at Sylvia, who came to her rescue explaining her history.

Madame kissed her.

"You are the first compatriot of mine to come to my school. I will make a good dancer of you. Yes?"

Petrova scratched at the floor with her toe and said nothing; she daren't look up, for she was sure Pauline would make her laugh.

"And this is Posy," said Sylvia.

Posy came forward and dropped the most beautiful curtsy.

"Madame," she said politely.

"Blessed lamb!" Nana whispered proudly.

"Little show-off!" Pauline whispered to Petrova.

Madame sent for Theo and told her to take them to the classroom, and they went into the junior dancing class. Here about twenty small girls in royal-blue rompers and white socks and black patent-leather shoes were learning tap-dancing. Theo spoke to the teacher. Madame, she said, wanted to see what classes to put these three children into. Madame sat down, and Sylvia and Nana sat beside her. The twenty little girls settled down cross-legged on the floor. Theo took the children to the middle of the room and told the pianist to play a simple polka. Then she began to dance.

"You dance too, dears," she said.

Pauline turned crimson. She had seen the sort of thing the twenty children in the class were doing, and she knew that she could do nothing like that, and that they were all younger than she was.

"Dance, Pauline dear," Theo said. "Copy me."

Pauline gave an agonized look at Sylvia, who smiled sympathy and encouragement, then she held out the skirts of her smock and began to polka.

"Thank goodness we all know how to do this one," she thought. "We should have looked fools if it had been a waltz."

Petrova began to polka straight away, but she did it very badly, stumbling over her feet.

"I won't mind," she said to herself. "I know I can't dance like all those children, so it's no good trying."

She would not look at them though, for she was sure they were whispering about her.

Posy was delighted to hear the music. Theo had taught her to polka and she was charmed to show it off. She picked up her feet and held out her skirts, and pointed her toes; she thought it great fun.

"Just look at Posy!" Pauline whispered to Petrova as she passed her.

Petrova looked, and wished she could do it like that.

"Stop," said Theo. "Come here, dear."

She took hold of the children one by one and lifted first their right legs and then their left over their heads. Then she left them and went to Madame Fidolia. She curtsied.

"Elementary, Madame?"

Madame got up; as she did so, all the children rose off the floor.

"Elementary," she said. She shook first Sylvia and then Nana by the hand. "Good-bye, children."

She turned to go, and all the twenty children and the pianist and the instructress and Theo curtsied, saying "Madame" in reverent voices. Pauline, Petrova and Posy did it too, but a little late. Sylvia gave rather a deep bow, and Nana a bob.

"Well," said Nana, as the door closed, "if you ask

me, it's for all the world like taking dancing classes in Buckingham Palace."

"That's very satisfactory," Theo explained to Sylvia. "The elementary classes are from four to five every afternoon. The acting classes are on Saturdays, so that all the children can be brought together. It will be more difficult later on, when they are in different classes."

They went home on a bus.

"Do you know," Pauline whispered to Petrova as they sat down together on the front seat on the top, "that soon it's Posy's birthday, when we have to do our vows again, and we can't."

"Why not?"

"Well, didn't we vow to make Fossil a name in history books? Whoever heard of people on the stage in history books?"

"We needn't be actresses always, though," Petrova said comfortingly. "I asked Mr. Simpson, and he said because you were a thing from the time you were twelve till you grew up it didn't mean you had to be it always."

"It's difficult to see how to be in a history book, anyway," Pauline said, in a worried sort of voice. "It's mostly Kings and Queens who are. People like Princess

Elizabeth will be; but not us whatever we did—at least, it will be difficult."

"There's Joan of Arc." Petrova tried to remember a few more names. "I know there were a lot, but I didn't get as far as a whole reign, I was only doing 'Tales from History' when we left Cromwell House. Then I did that little bit about Alfred the Great with Garnie; and Doctor Jakes hasn't given me a history lesson yet. But there were lots. I know there were. We'll ask Doctor Jakes to tell us about them."

Sylvia leaned over from the seat behind.

"Look, darlings, here is a shilling. I want you all to have cakes for tea to make up for a very hard-working afternoon."

V

The Children's Academy of Dancing

*

THE FOSSILS became some of the busiest children in London. They got up at half-past seven and had breakfast at eight. After breakfast they did exercises with Theo for half an hour. At nine they began lessons. Posy did two hours' reading, writing, and kindergarten work with Sylvia, and Pauline and Petrova did three hours with Doctor Jakes and Doctor Smith. They were very interesting lessons, but terribly hard work; for if Doctor Smith was teaching Pauline, Doctor Jakes taught Petrova, and the other way on, and as both doctors had spent their lives coaching people for terribly stiff examinations—though of course they taught quite easy things to the children—they never got the idea out of their minds that a stiff examination was a thing everybody had to pass some day. There was a little break of ten minutes in the middle of the morning when milk and biscuits were brought in; but after a day or two they were never eaten or drunk. Both doctors had lovely ideas about the sort of things to have in the middle of lessons—a meal they called a beaver.

They took turns to get it ready. Sometimes it was chocolate with cream on it, and sometimes Doctor Jakes' ginger drink, and once it was ice-cream soda; and the things to eat were never the same: queer biscuits, little ones from Japan with delicate flowers painted on them in sugar, cakes from Vienna, and specialties of different kinds from all over England. They had their beavers sitting round the fire in either of the doctors' rooms, and they had discussions which had nothing to do with lessons. At twelve o'clock they went for a walk with Nana or Sylvia. They liked it best when Sylvia took them. She had better ideas about walks; she thought the Park the place to go to, and thought it a good idea to take hoops and things to play with. Nana liked a nice clean walk up as far as the Victoria and Albert and back. On wet days Sylvia thought it a good plan to stay in and make toffee or be read out loud to. Nana thought nicely brought-up children ought to be out of the house between twelve and one, even on a wet day, and she took them to see the dolls' houses in the Victoria and Albert. The children liked the dolls' houses; but there are a lot of wet days in the winter, and they saw them a good deal. Pauline and Petrova had lunch with Sylvia, Posy had hers with Nana. After lunch they all had to take a book on their beds for half an hour. In the afternoons

there was another walk, this one always with Nana.
It lasted an hour, and as they had usually walked to
the Victoria and Albert in the morning, they did not
have to go there again, but took turns to choose where
they went. Pauline liked walking where there were
shops. Petrova liked the Earl's Court Road, because
there were three motor showrooms for her to look at.
Posy liked to go towards the King's Road, Chelsea,
because on the way they passed a shop that sold pup-
pies. They all liked Posy's walk; but they did not
choose it themselves because they knew she would. If
Nana was not so sure that they must save the penny
and walk they would have gone to much more exciting
places; for you can't get far on your legs when there is
only an hour, and that includes getting home again.
Tea was in the nursery at a quarter to four, and at half
past they went by the Piccadilly railway to Russell
Square. They all liked going on the underground; but
both Gloucester Road, where they got in, and Russell
Square, where they got out, were those mean sort of
stations that have lifts instead of moving staircases.

"Going to dancing class," Petrova said almost every
day, "wouldn't be so bad if only there was even one
moving staircase."

As soon as they got to the Academy they went
down to the changing-room. There they shared a

locker in which their rompers and practice-frocks and shoes were kept. Their rompers were royal blue with C.A. for Children's Academy embroidered on the pockets. They wore their rompers for the first half-hour, and with them white socks and black patent-leather ankle-strapped shoes. In these clothes they did exercises and a little dancing which was known as "character", and twice a week they worked at tap dancing. At the end of half an hour they hung towels round their necks (for they were supposed to get so hot they would need a wipe down) and went back to the changing-room and put on their white tarlatan practice-frocks. These were like overalls with no join down the back; the bodice had hooks and the frills of the skirt wrapped over and clipped. With this they wore white socks and white kid slippers. The work they did in these dresses they found dull, and it made their legs ache. They did not realize that the half-hour spent holding on to a bar and doing what they thought stupid exercises was very early training for ballet. Ballet to them meant wearing blocked shoes like the little pair that had come with Posy or such as the more advanced classes wore at school. Sometimes Madame Fidolia came in to watch their class, and directly she arrived they all let go of the practice-bar and curtsied to the floor saying "Madame".

They got home at half-past six, and Posy went straight to bed. Sylvia read to the other two for twenty minutes, and then Petrova had to go up, and at seven, Pauline. The lights were out by half-past and there was no more talking.

On Saturday mornings they worked from ten to one at the Academy. As well as special exercise classes and the ordinary dancing classes, there was singing, and one hour's acting class. For these they wore the Academy overalls. They were of black sateen made from a Russian design, with high collars, and double-breasted, buttoning with large black buttons down the left side; round the waist they had wide black leather belts. With these they wore their white sandals.

Petrova, who hated clothes, found the everlasting changing an awful bore. Saturdays were the worst.

"Oh, I do hate Saturdays," she said to Nana. "I get up in my jersey and skirt, and as soon as I get to the Academy I change everything, even put a vest on instead of my combinations, and wear those rompers; and then my practice-dress and the overall; and then back into my combinations and my skirt and jersey. I wish I was a savage and wore nothing."

"That's no way to talk," Nana told her severely. "Many a poor little child would be glad of the nice clothes you wear; and as for changing out of your combies, I'm glad you do; you wear holes in them fast enough without all that dancing in them."

From the very beginning Madame took an interest in Posy. Each class that she came to watch she made her do some step alone. Posy had her shoes taken off one day and her instep looked at; Madame was so delighted at the shape and flexibility of her feet that she called the rest of the class to look at them. The rest of the class admired them while Madame was there, but secretly none of them could see anything about them different from their own. Pauline and Petrova thought it very bad for Posy to be made so conspicuous, and to teach her not to get cocky they called her "Posy-Pretty-Toes" all the way home. Posy hated it and at last burst into tears. Nana was very cross.

"That's right, you two, tease poor little Posy; she can't help Madame saying she has nice feet. It's jealous, that's what you are. Any more of your nonsense and you'll go to bed half an hour early."

"Why should we be jealous?" asked Petrova. "Who cares what feet look like? They are just useful things."

Pauline giggled.

"Have you pretty feet, Nana?" She looked down at Nana's square-toed black shoes which she always wore.

"I have what God gave me," Nana said reverently, "and they're all I need, never having thoughts to dance in a ballet."

The thought of Nana, who was very fat, dancing in a ballet made them all laugh so much that they forgot to call Posy "Pretty-Toes" again, and they were still laughing when they got home.

It was at the acting classes that Pauline shone. The acting in their first term was entirely in mime. They acted whole fairy stories without saying a word. Whether she was a princess, or a peasant, or an old man, Pauline managed to make them real without any dressing up, but just in the way she moved.

At singing classes none of them shone. They could keep in tune, except Posy, who could not hear one note from another. But that was all—they were in no way distinguished.

Just before Christmas the school broke up for a month. All the senior girls were working in panto-mimes, and for some time all those who were not old enough for licenses had felt very unimportant. The children's classes were moved from one room to another to make room for rehearsals, and the notice-board was covered with rehearsal calls. "All concerned in the Rose Ballet, in room three at 4.30." "The children appearing in 'Red Riding Hood,' 5.30, room seven."

"The principals for the Jewel Ballet 4 o'clock, room one." And, as well, calls for the children stars. "Poppy: 10.30 with Madame Fidolia." "Winifred: 12 o'clock with Madame Fidolia."

Pauline, Petrova, and Posy would gaze in great awe at these names.

"Winifred," one of them would say—"that's the girl who wears a fur coat. Poppy is going to be 'Alice in Wonderland'. She's the one with the long hair."

They would peep through the glass on the doors of the rooms where the rehearsals were taking place, and stare at the children who were already twelve and old enough to earn money.

"Not this Christmas, but the one after I shall be one of those children," Pauline said enviously.

"Do you want to be?" Petrova asked in surprise. "I'm very glad I'm not twelve, except because of Garnie wanting money to look after us."

Pauline watched the figures through the glass, the rows of white practice-dresses, and the rows of pink canvas ballet shoes.

"I don't want to be them, exactly," she explained, "but I want to be me old enough not to dance, but to act. I'd like that."

Posy could not see through the glass without standing on her toes. Suddenly watching the ballet rehearsal she got up on to her points. She was only wearing her sandals, but she did not seem worried by the position. Pauline nudged Petrova.

"Look at Posy."

Petrova looked. Then both of them tried to stand up on their toes, but they could not—it hurt. Posy was not looking at them; but she lolled against the door balanced on her points as easily as if they were her flat feet. Petrova said at last:

"Could you walk on your toes like that, Posy?"

Posy looked down at her feet as if surprised at the way they were behaving. Then she walked down the passage. She was perfectly easy on her points, as though it was ordinary to walk on them. Pauline and Petrova did not show her how impressed they were, as they thought it would be bad for her. But on the way home Pauline said:

"You know, Petrova, I do think Posy really has got rather nice little feet."

Petrova nodded.

"I shouldn't wonder if she danced terribly well."

At the end of the term Sylvia was told that the children would work differently in future. Pauline was to move into a more advanced class for everything, and to come to an extra class for acting in French on Wednesdays and Fridays. Posy was to give up all acting and singing, and to take fencing instead, and all her classes in future were to be given by Madame herself. Posy was too small to be impressed at the plans for her future; but not only Pauline and Petrova were impressed for her, but the whole Academy. She was the only child since the school had started that Madame had picked out from the baby class to come entirely under her supervision.

"Do you know," Pauline told Nana, "these afternoons since the school heard about Posy quite big girls come to watch our class. The ones who are old enough to have a license."

"I daresay. Let's hope it won't turn her head. You've done very well too, Pauline. One of the mothers of a child in your class I was talking to told me her little girl had been in that same class three terms."

"That's what I'll be, I expect," Petrova said gloomily.

Nana was consoling.

"I wouldn't fret, dear; we can't all have the same gifts."

Petrova was very depressed, though. She did not want to be a good dancer; but since she had to dance at all it was annoying to see someone younger than herself doing so much better; and then Pauline moving up was a blow, as it left her alone in her class. Pauline had often helped her with steps at home so that she did not get on too badly; but with Pauline gone she was suspicious that she might be the dunce of the class.

It was Christmas when the term ended. The children at once settled down to making paper rings, which, when they were finished, Mr. Simpson hung all over the house. On Christmas Eve Mrs. Simpson and Sylvia put holly over the pictures, and mistletoe on to the lamp in the hall. The two doctors had secrets going on in their rooms that they would not tell anyone, and nobody could go in. Cook and Clara were busy in the kitchen all day long, and told the children they were not to come down. Only Theo was not there. She was away up in Manchester putting final touches to the dances of a group of children from the Academy who were appearing in the pantomime.

Pauline and Petrova were with Sylvia while Posy was going to bed.

"There is a lovely feeling about Christmas Eve," Pauline said. "My inside almost hurts being excited; I can't sit still for wishing it was tomorrow."

Sylvia smiled.

"You deserve a nice Christmas, darlings. You have been such hard-working children all the term; I want you to have lovely holidays."

"It's a lovely holiday just not having to go to the Academy," Petrova pointed out.

Sylvia looked worried.

"Do you hate it so?"

Petrova was just going to say how much she loathed it when Pauline kicked her, and she remembered how Theo had told them that they would be able to help by earning money. She flushed.

"No, I don't. It's quite fun really." She spoke as much as if she meant it as she could.

Sylvia gave a thankful sigh.

"I'm so glad! I wouldn't let any of you do it unless you were happy."

Nana came to the door.

"Do you know it's nearly seven, Petrova, and your bath getting cold, and a big stocking of mine waiting for you to hang up."

"Stockings!" Pauline jumped up. "I shall come to bed now too, Nana, to make it quicker to get to Christmas morning."

VI

Petrova Has Influenza and Makes a Friend

*

PERHAPS because they had been working so hard, Christmas day seemed the loveliest they had known. Nothing was very different from other Christmases; but somehow it seemed a particularly gay day. Their stockings bulged when they woke, and besides all the usual things in them, there were large white sugar pigs with pink noses and wool tails. When Nana came to tell them to get up, she had three parcels under her arm, and they, of course, had presents for her. Pauline had made her some handkerchiefs, and Petrova a needle-book full of needles, and Posy a blotter of two plaited paper mats stuck on cardboard. Nana had knitted each of them a jumper with fluffy rabbit's wool round the cuffs and collars. Pauline's was blue, Petrova's orange, and Posy's pink. They all put them on for breakfast. On the breakfast table were chocolates for them from Theo; everybody else's presents were waiting for the Christmas tree after tea. They went to church—even Posy—and sang "Hark, the Herald Angels," "Oh Come, all Ye Faithful," and "The

First Nöel". They had been afraid that perhaps they would only get one that they knew and the rest some dull tune that was supposed to belong to Christmas and did not really. The turkey and plum pudding and crystallized fruits and things they had for lunch, as Posy was not allowed to sit up to dinner. After lunch Sylvia read to them while they did an enormous jig-saw that she had got especially for Christmas afternoon. Then there was tea, and Cook had made a most re-markable cake with a Father Christmas and reindeer on it, and also three large gold stars which she said was what she hoped the children would be.

It was when they went into Doctor Smith's room for the Christmas tree that they had the big surprise of the day. Sylvia always had a Christmas tree for them; but this was not like any tree they had seen before. It was the usual fir tree; but every branch was covered with glittering frost, which made the tree shine as though it were magic.

"Was that what you were doing when you were both locked in yesterday?" Pauline asked the doctors.

They agreed that it was, and seemed very pleased that everyone thought it so beautiful. Cook said it was as pretty as a picture, and Clara that it put her in mind of something off a Christmas card, and Nana that it was very nice indeed, but she was glad nobody was expecting her to stick all that stuff on the branches. Mrs. Simpson said that she and Mr. Simpson were very lucky that it was so lovely a tree on the Christmas day that they were home, as they didn't have a Christmas tree in Kuala Lumpur. Sylvia told the two doctors if that was how Christmas trees ought to look, they would always have to stay in the house, because she knew she couldn't decorate them like that. The three children thought it so perfectly beautiful that they could not say anything at all, but just walked round and round it admiring.

The Christmas presents were very satisfactory; but everybody else's faded into unimportance beside Sylvia's. She gave them each a jewel-box, and when they were opened they had wrist watches inside. Pauline's on a blue strap, Petrova's on a white, and Posy's on a pink. In the boxes with them was a plain brown strap for ordinary days.

"Garnie! Just to match Gum's necklaces," Pauline exclaimed, so excited that she could not fasten the strap, and Mrs. Simpson had to do it for her.

The children were wearing white organdie dresses with Gum's necklaces and sashes to match them, except Petrova's, which was a scarlet sash. Everybody agreed the watches were just the right finishing touch.

Petrova was as pleased as the others, but a bit worried.

"Weren't they dreadfully expensive, Garnie?" she whispered.

She knew it was the rudest thing you could do to ask the price of a present, but she could not bear to think that Sylvia had made herself poorer than ever buying watches.

Sylvia drew her into a corner.

"I'll tell you a secret. I had a great big gold watch that had been my father's. I couldn't use it, so I sold it and bought those for you. So in a way they didn't cost anything at all."

After the last present had been opened and the last candle on the tree blown out, they played charades and hide-and-seek all over the house. It was all great fun; but everybody suddenly thought about the time. This was the end, and Christmas day was over for another year, which was a miserable feeling. Presently Cook and Clara went away to get dressed for their own Christmas party downstairs, and then Nana took Posy to bed. After that, although they had supper of cold turkey and meringues, the day was terribly finished, and both Pauline and Petrova felt as though they had been balloons, but were now pricked and had gone flat. Then suddenly a lovely thing happened. A large choir of carol-singers came under the window and sang. They all leaned out to hear, and it was like a play. The singers, both men and women, wore masks and colored capes and hoods, and they carried lanterns. They sang most beautifully "God rest you Merry Gentlemen," and "The Holly and the Ivy," and "Sleep, Holy Babe". Pauline and Petrova took a plate each and collected money for them. Pauline did best, because she went to the kitchen, where the party was, and Petrova went to the nursery where there was only Nana and Posy; but with what the boarders and Sylvia gave them, and their own pennies, they had nearly fifteen shillings. Sylvia made them put on their coats, and Mr. Simpson opened the front door for them, and they took the money out. The singers were just finishing the last verse of "Sleep, Holy Babe". They waited till they had done, then they gave them the money. They were very pleased, and thought fifteen shillings a wonderful lot to have got; they said the money was all going to a children's hospital. They asked if Pauline and Petrova would like to choose a carol before they went to another street. Pauline thought a moment, and before she had done thinking Petrova said—"Oh, please, 'Like Silver Lamps'," so they sang that one.

That was the end of the day, when the carol was

finished, and they called out "Thank you. A happy Christmas," for Nana was waiting to take them up to bed. They did not mind the day being over nearly as much as they had before the carol-singers came, because they had made such a lovely finish to it.

The Christmas holidays went terribly fast. They did a lot of nice things; but the nicest of all was going to a pantomime in which all the children dancing in it came from the Academy. They found it very difficult not to whisper every time the children came on because they wanted to point out to each other that: "The one two from the end is that girl that came on the tube with us. . . ." and "That one with the black hair in the middle is the one who has a sister in our class". They felt very grand when they got home being able to say to Mr. and Mrs. Simpson and the two doctors that there were a lot of "our girls" in the pantomime.

The spring term at the Academy both Pauline and Posy loved, and Petrova hated. Pauline was given two real parts to learn, one as "Cinderella" in French, a play of the fairy story called "Cendrillon", and the other as "Tyltyl" in some scenes from "The Blue Bird": In the intermediate dancing class, although it was not till the end of the term that she used her points, she wore real ballet shoes. Theo Dane taught this class, which made it extra nice.

Posy, after she joined Madame's dancing class, seemed to get very grown-up for somebody who would not be seven until September. She said she did not do a great many exercises at her lessons, that a lot of the time Madame told her things. Asked what things, she could only say vaguely, "Just things". She was always dancing. Sometimes in the nursery, which did not matter, but sometimes in the road, which Nana did not approve of at all, and once on the tube station, which Pauline and Petrova thought frightful showing off; for Posy was very noticeable, with her red hair, and she already danced rather well for somebody of her age, and people stared.

"You are a show-off, Posy," Pauline said.

"It's not showing off, it's because I thought of something and wanted to see if my feet would do it," Posy explained.

"You could wait till you get home, couldn't you?" Petrova grumbled, for she hated people looking at them.

"I might have forgotten," Posy argued. Then she danced again.

"Make her stop, Nana," Petrova implored.

"That's enough, Posy," Nana said sharply. "Dancing on a railway station, indeed; we shall have people asking us where the organ is, for we seem to have got a monkey."

Posy stopped, not because she cared what Nana or the others thought, but because her feet had done what she wanted them to do. Both Pauline and Petrova then, and lots of times, had a feeling that she was not proud of her dancing, but looked on it as something that mattered more than anything else. She thought that doing an exercise beautifully mattered so much, that in spite of feeling that it was silly to let somebody of six think what she did mattered, they had an odd feeling that she was right.

Petrova hated her classes. Not because she was the dunce of the class, for she was not. Left to herself without Pauline to practice with her she learnt all the exercises as easily as any of the other children; but the truth was she disliked dancing. This term's work was almost all exercises, half of them done at the bar; and she had the sense to see that she would not like the work more as she moved higher up the school. The more efficient you became, the longer hours you were expected to work, and the more exercises you had to do. She felt very depressed because she had no one much to talk to about it. Pauline was so happy at the Academy that it was no good hoping she would understand, and Posy was not only too young to talk to, but thought dancing the only thing that mattered in the world.

She could not say a word to Sylvia, because she knew it would be a help when she was old enough to earn money, nor to Nana, who had an idea that the reason she did not get on as well as the others was because she had "always been such a one for playing about like a boy". The only person she could talk to was Mr. Simpson, and she did not see much of him. When she did he was grand; he thought just as she did—that dancing was rather stupid, and cars and things much more important.

"Hullo, Petrova!" he would call up the stairs sometimes on Sunday afternoons, "having a bit of trouble with the car. Come and give me a hand."

The most gorgeous afternoons followed; he was not the sort of man who did everything himself and expected you to watch, but took turns fairly, passing over the spanner, saying "Here, you take those nuts off". Of course she used to get most terribly dirty; but Mrs. Simpson always prepared for that by putting an old mackintosh, which she had cut down, on top of whatever Petrova was wearing, and she made her wash and inspected her carefully before Nana saw her. Neither Petrova nor Mr. Simpson talked much while they were working; but he got to know quite a lot about how she felt.

"How's the dancing been this week?" he would ask.

"Awful."

"Still doing nothing but exercises?"

"Yes. Battlements—always battlements."

She meant Battement, but she had only heard the word and never seen it written, and had got it wrong, and of course Mr. Simpson did not know one dancing term from another.

"Battlements," he murmured. Then he laughed. "Silly words they use at your dancing."

The moment he laughed she felt better. If even one person like Mr. Simpson did not think dancing mattered terribly, perhaps it did not.

Just before the end of the term Petrova had influenza. She had the worst kind, that is gastric, and makes you sick all day. She felt so miserable for a week that she did not care about anything. Nana looked after her, and Sylvia took the other two to their classes, helped by Mr. Simpson and his car. At the end of a week Petrova woke up one morning suddenly better. Her head had stopped going round and round, and her inside felt itself again.

"What can I have for breakfast, Nana?" she asked. "I'm awfully hungry."

Nana felt her hands with an experienced air and nodded.

"No temperature this morning. That's a good girl. What about a boiled egg?"

She went away and cooked it, and brought the tray and put it down on the bed-table over Petrova's knees. Then she laid down a large bundle of papers.

"That Mr. Simpson sent you those," she said. "He's clearing out, and this lot he said you'd like."

Petrova looked at the papers. They were all about cars and aeroplanes, and she would like them; but she did not like the expression "clearing out". It made her inside feel as if it was going down in a lift.

"Are they going back to Kuala Lumpur?"

"That's right." Nana straightened the eiderdown. "Miss Brown will have to be looking for some new boarders."

"Oh." Petrova laid down her egg-spoon. Suddenly she was not hungry after all. "I don't think I want this egg, Nana."

"Now, you come on and eat it."

Nana sat down beside her and began opening the magazines, and asked such silly questions about the aeroplanes that Petrova had to put her right, and talking, she ate her egg without noticing. Nana might be stupid about aeroplanes, but she was very good at getting people to eat when they did not want to.

The first day out of bed when you have had gastric influenza is not nice. Everybody is the same. They say "Can't I get up?" and then at last they do get up, and they wish they were back in bed. That is exactly how it was with Petrova. Nana got her up about lunch-time, and moved her on to a sofa in the day nursery, and she left her there when she took the others out in the afternoon. Petrova looked through the window and watched them all walk up the Cromwell Road, and thought how miserable everything was. The Simpsons going away, and the Dancing Academy, and she laid down on the sofa and cried like anything. While she was crying and had got to that stage when all your words run together, and your nose is as if it was in the worst stages of a cold, and your face comes out in red lumps, there was a knock on the door. She stopped a sob to say "Come in", but all that came out was "Cubin," and that was so indistinct that nobody could have heard it. So the knock came again, and this time waited for no answer; but the door opened and in walked Mr. Simpson. He did not do anything idiotic like pretending not to see that Petrova was howling, but instead sat down and laughed.

"That's exactly what I want to do after influenza. Have my handkerchief." He passed it over. "It's new and it's clean, and has beautiful initials embroidered on it."

Petrova took it, and after a lot of blowing and mopping, felt better. She looked at the initials on the handkerchief.

"They are nice," she said stuffily. "What's the J. for?"

"John."

"Is your name John? Nana would like that; it's after an apostle like me and Pauline." She gave the handkerchief back.

He put it in his pocket.

"Do you think it would make you feel better to hear my troubles?"

She nodded.

"Well, I can't go back to Kuala Lumpur."

"Why?"

"A thing called a slump."

She looked puzzled.

"What's a slump?"

He thought a moment, and then explained that it was as if, after training for years to be a dancer, she grew up to find that there were thousands of children all trained to dance, so there were more than were wanted, and none of them could earn anything. His rubber trees were like that.

"Thousands more of them than are wanted?"

"That's right, and cheaper things than rubber trees found to get rubber from."

"Do you mean you won't go back to Kuala Lumpur ever?"

"Probably not." He smiled at her because she looked so pleased. "I'm glad somebody thinks it good news."

"Will you just go on living here and doing nothing?"

"Not nothing, no. I have bought a garage."

"Oh!" Petrova was quite pink with excitement. "Where?"

"It's a big one not far from Piccadilly. I hope to make lots of money out of it."

"Will you go on living with us?"

"I hope so. I thought on Sunday afternoons and in the holidays you might come along and lend a hand."

"In a real garage?"

Petrova could not believe her luck. Suddenly nothing mattered: dancing classes, or having influenza—everything looked gay. She got off the sofa, and her legs, instead of feeling like cotton wool as they had all the morning, felt strong enough to go for a walk. She put her arms round his neck.

"When can I go and see it?"

He stood up so that she had to curl her legs round his waist to hold on. He carried her through the door like that.

"Tomorrow morning if it's fine I am taking you there in the car; but you are only to be out for half an hour. Now I am taking you down to tea with us. My wife has spent the whole morning thinking of things people might like to eat after having influenza."

VII

Maeterlinck's "Blue Bird"

*

THE SUMMER term at the Academy was fun. For two whole terms they had done nothing much but exercises, and though Pauline played parts in the acting class, there had been no dressing-up. Then one morning just before the term began, Sylvia got a letter asking them all to come to tea at the Academy, as Madame had something she wanted to talk about. There was a P.S. to the letter to say "The students will wear formal dress". None of them knew which dress "formal" was; but Theo said it meant overalls. They all thought this most peculiar, as you cannot think of anything less formal than an overall. They were all very excited to know what the meeting was about. Theo, who knew, would not say.

"You wait, you'll hear soon enough."

Pauline tugged at her hand.

"Is it nice?"

Theo thought a moment.

"It's to do with happiness. It means hard work."

They all tried to guess what she meant by that; but

they could not, and she would not say another word.

On the day of the meeting Mr. Simpson drove them to the Academy. Sylvia went in at the middle door marked "emy of Dancing an", the children and Nana in at the students' entrance under "Children's Acad", and Theo in at the staff entrance in the third house marked "d Stage Training".

They all met in the big main hall which ran through all three houses. It was not looking a bit like it looked on ordinary days. There was a platform with a lot of chairs and a table on it, and flowers standing in pots round it. There was tea laid out on the tables down the side, and rows of chairs at the bottom of the room for the grown-up people. The students stood until Madame came in and they had all given her their usual greeting, then they were told to sit cross-legged on the floor. Madame was looking as different as possible from how she looked in term time. Instead of her practice-dress she wore a really smart black satin frock; it was made a little like the school overalls, only very well cut. All her staff were with her, not looking themselves at all either; except Miss Catherine Jay, who had been a well-known actress, and was now head of the acting school, and her two assistants, Miss Brown and Miss Webb, also Madame Moulin, who taught acting in French. Those four usually looked quite nice;

but the children had never seen the dancing teachers, except Theo, in anything but a grown-up edition of their own practice-dresses. When Madame came forward to speak there was an excited movement; for of course everyone wanted to know why they had been asked to tea. She started her speech by telling them how hard the lives of many Russians had been since the revolution, and, with so many poor of their own, how difficult it had been for other countries to take in penniless refugees. Then she told the story of one family that had come to England. She said that the mother had died, but work had been given the father, and how the three little girls had gone to an ordinary State school, and had begun to learn English and were getting on nicely, when the youngest, Olga, developed a serious illness. Careful nursing, good feeding, and good doctoring would be needed over a long time if she was ever to get better. What was the father to do? Olga's illness was not one that a hospital would willingly take, would be in bed for such a while, and a bed over a long period could not easily be spared. She could be nursed at home, but where was the money to come from for medicines and special food? By the laws of England the two other girls must attend school, and in any case the eldest, Maria, was only ten.

"It was then," said Madame, "that friends came to

me and told me their story. It happened that I had met a man attached as head surgeon to a great children's hospital. I told him about Olga; he said something must be done. What was done, children, was that they took her in, they kept her in the hospital for over six months, and then they sent her away to the country for nearly six months more, and she came back completely well." Madame smiled. "Before I go on I know you will want to know where she is now. She is a hospital nurse in the very children's hospital that cured her." Madame leaned on the table and her face grew serious. "Two weeks ago Olga came to me. 'Madame,' she said, 'the hospital needs money; it has to be moved into the country. I have done what I can to help, but it is very little.' Then she turned to me with her hands out and said, 'Madame, will you help the hospital as once you helped me?' Children, what could I say?"

None of the children were very certain if this was a real question, or the sort of one people first asked and then answered themselves, so only a very muttered "Yes" was heard; but of course they all knew that she must have said "yes"—what else could she say? Madame looked round the hall as if to be certain that everyone was listening.

"My children, my guests, I have asked you here

this afternoon to put the same question to you. Will you help the hospital that once helped Olga?"

She did not wait for an answer this time, but went on to explain what she meant. They had been lent a theater for a matinée at the end of July, and she intended to give a performance of "The Blue Bird". All her old students had offered to help—they would play and dance all the grown-up roles; but the school would have to provide, besides Tyltyl and Mytyl, Stars and Hours and Unborn Children, and a lot of other things. This would not only mean a considerable amount of work for the children, but a lot of clothes. She was going to ask everybody present who would help to stand up. The parents, if they would provide and make the dresses, and the children, if they would give the extra work.

Of course everybody stood up, and then one of the senior girls asked what everybody wanted to know. She gave a deep curtsy.

"Madame, who are to be Tyltyl and Mytyl?"

Madame nodded.

"Of course you all want to know that. Miss Jay and I have decided that Pauline Fossil shall play Tyltyl. The two children must be petite, and she has been working at the part for a whole term already. The child who has played Mytyl all last term has unfortunately got measles, so we have decided to try Pauline's sister Petrova, because it will be easy for the two to work together." Then she waved to the tea. "Will you please all come and eat."

Madame served tea to the grown-up people out of a samovar. The children had tea out of ordinary tea-pots, poured out for them by the teachers. Pauline and Petrova felt very red about the face. Half the school did not know them by sight and others had to point them out, and more people came over and asked them if they were Pauline and Petrova, and told them how lucky they were. Just before they left, Theo told them to go and speak to Madame.

Madame was still sitting in front of her samovar. As soon as they had given their curtsies, she put an arm round each of them.

"Pauline, Madame Jay gives me a very good account of your work in her class, that is why I am trusting Tyltyl to you." Then she looked at Petrova. "I am very anxious that you should be sufficiently good to play Mytyl, not only because, being sisters, it will make rehearsals easy, but because you are also Russian, and so have an especial debt to the hospital for its goodness to one of your countrywomen."

Both Pauline and Petrova stammered out something about meaning to work very hard; but Petrova thought to herself, that though of course she was very glad to help the hospital, it was not because she was Russian; for she was British by adoption, and had taken a British name, and felt very British inside.

They went home on the tube, and Pauline told them all the story of "The Blue Bird", as she was the only one who knew it.

"It's about two children," she explained, "called Tyltyl and Mytyl. Tyltyl is a boy and Mytyl a girl."

"That's a pity," Nana interrupted: "with your hair you'd make the better girl, and Petrova the boy."

Pauline shook her head.

"The boy's the eldest, and has most to say. It tells all the places they go to look for a blue bird which really means happiness."

"Did they find a blue bird?" Posy asked.

"Yes. It was at their home all the time. Tyltyl's dove. It was blue, but they'd never noticed."

"Where do we look for it?" Petrova wanted to know.

"In the Land of Memory; that's where the children's grandfather and grandmother and their brothers and sisters who have died, live. And with Night. And amongst the children who aren't born. And with the dead people. In the end Tyltyl's dove flies away, and Tyltyl says to the people who are watching the play:

'If any of you should find him, would you be so very kind as to give him back to us? . . . We need him for our happiness, later on. . . .' "

If it had not been for Doctor Jakes, Petrova would not have kept the part of Mytyl. Naturally, in a school training children to be professional actresses and dancers, a high standard was not only expected, but insisted on. Three days after the rehearsal of any scene the children had to be word-perfect, and might not open their books even when off stage. At the rehearsals, before they had to be word-perfect, every single move that they made had to be written into their books, and learnt with their parts; and the stage manager at the same time wrote it into her book, and there it was, a part of the prompt copy, and even half a step taken when no move was down to be made caused trouble. Of course they had to speak the exact script. No little word, even "an" or a "the", could be wrong. Both Madame and Miss Jay said that an author wrote down what he or she wanted said, and no actor, amateur or professional, had a right to alter the words in any way whatsoever.

None of these things would have worried Petrova. If you know you have got to learn a thing by heart and that it has to be absolutely accurate, any child can learn it: it is only a matter of concentrating. Acting the part when you have learnt it is a different matter. Pauline had a natural gift for saying a line right. Petrova could just as easily say a line wrong. If she had been left to learn the part of Mytyl only at the Academy rehearsals, she could not have done it. Except in the first scene, and the graveyard scene, when she and Pauline were alone on the stage, there were always the grown-ups, for all the "things" that accompanied the children on their search for the blue bird were played by ex-students, some of them very distinguished ones.

Petrova, already shy and nervous, would have been quite unable to remember her words, or how to say them in front of these people, if it had not been for Doctor Jakes. With lessons all the mornings and rehearsals from four to six every day, and from ten to one on Saturdays, it was not easy to find time to work with her; but somehow it was squeezed in. She had the half-hour after breakfast that had been the time when Theo took them all for extra exercises, and she managed to steal half an hour out of lesson time most days. She believed that nobody could say a line wrong if they thought what they were saying. She believed, too, that it was quite easy to behave like a natural child on the stage if you thought all the time so hard that you forgot yourself. In the opening of "The Blue

Bird", where the children are in bed, Petrova found it difficult to forget that she was Petrova sitting on a sofa meant to be a bed, rehearsing a part, and to think only that she was Mytyl, the daughter of a poor woodcutter.

Tyltyl.   Mytyl?

Mytyl.   Tyltyl?

Tyltyl.   Are you asleep?

Mytyl.   Are you? . . .

Tyltyl.   No; how can I be asleep when I'm talking to you?

Mytyl.   I say, is this Christmas Day? . . .

Tyltyl.   Not yet; not till tomorrow. But Father Christmas won't bring us anything this year. . . .

Mytyl.   Why not?

Tyltyl.   I heard Mummy say that she couldn't go to town to tell him. . . . But he will come next year.

Mytyl.   Is next year far off? . . .

Tyltyl.   A good long while. . . . But he will come to the rich children tonight. . . .

Mytyl.   Really? . . .

Tyltyl.   Hullo! . . . Mummy's forgotten to put out the lamp! . . . I've an idea! . . .

* From *The Blue Bird* by Maurice Maeterlinck. Copyright, 1907–1935, by Dodd, Mead & Company, Inc.

Mytyl. What?

Tyltyl. Let's get up. . . .

Mytyl. But we mustn't. . . .

Tyltyl. Why, there's no one about. . . . Do you see the shutters? . . .

Mytyl. Oh, how bright they are! . . .

Tyltyl. It's the lights of the party.

Mytyl. What party? . . .

Tyltyl. The rich children opposite. It's the Christmas-tree. Let's open the shutters. . . .

Mytyl. Can we? . . .

Tyltyl. Of course; there's no one to stop us. . . . Do you hear the music? . . . Let us get up. . . .

> [*The two* CHILDREN *get up, run to one of the windows, climb on to the stool and throw back the shutters. A bright light fills the room. The* CHILDREN *look out greedily.*]

Tyltyl. We can see everything! . . .

Mytyl (*who can hardly find room on the stool*). I can't. . . .

Tyltyl. It's snowing! . . . There's two carriages, with six horses each! . . .

Mytyl. There are twelve little boys getting out! . . .

Tyltyl. How silly you are! . . . They're little girls. . . .

Mytyl. They've got knickerbockers. . . .

Tyltyl. What do you know? . . . Don't push so: . . .

Mytyl. I never touched you.

Tyltyl (*who is taking up the whole stool*). You're taking up all the room. . . .

Mytyl. Why, I have no room at all! . . .

Tyltyl. Do be quiet: I see the tree! . . .

Mytyl. What tree? . . .

Tyltyl. Why, the Christmas-tree! . . . You're looking at the wall! . . .

Mytyl. I'm looking at the wall because I've got no room. . . .

Tyltyl (*giving her a miserly little place on the stool*). There! . . . Will that do? . . . Now you're better off than I! . . . I say, what lots and lots of lights! . . .

Mytyl. What are those people doing who are making such a noise? . . .

Tyltyl. They're the musicians.

Mytyl. Are they angry? . . .

Tyltyl. No; but it's hard work.

Mytyl. Another carriage with white horses! . . .

Tyltyl. Be quiet: . . . And look! . . .

Mytyl. What are those gold things there, hanging from the branches?

Tyltyl. Why, toys, to be sure! . . . Swords, guns, soldiers, cannons. . . .

Mytyl. And dolls; say, are there any dolls? . . .

Tyltyl. Dolls? . . . That's too silly; there's no fun in dolls. . . .

Mytyl. And what's that all round the table? . . .

Tyltyl. Cakes and fruit and tarts. . . .

Mytyl. I had some once when I was little. . . .

Tyltyl. So did I; it's nicer than bread, but they don't give you enough. . . .

Mytyl. They've got plenty over there. . . . The whole table's full. . . . Are they going to eat them? . . .

Tyltyl. Of course; what else would they do with them?

Mytyl. Why don't they eat them at once? . . .

Tyltyl. Because they're not hungry. . . .

Mytyl (*stupefied with astonishment*). Not hungry? . . . Why not? . . .

Tyltyl. Well, they eat whenever they want to. . . .

Mytyl (*incredulously*). Every day? . . .

Tyltyl. They say so. . . .

Mytyl. Will they eat them all? . . . Will they give any away? . . .

Tyltyl. To whom? . . .

Mytyl. To us. . . .

Tyltyl. They don't know us. . . .

Mytyl. Suppose we asked them. . . .

Tyltyl. We mustn't.

Mytyl. Why not? . . .

Tyltyl. Because it's not right.

Mytyl (*clapping her hands*). Oh, how pretty they are! . . .

Tyltyl (*rapturously*). And how they're laughing and laughing! . . .

Mytyl. And the little ones dancing! . . .

Tyltyl. Yes, yes; let's dance too! . . . (*They stamp their feet for joy on the stool.*)

Mytyl. Oh, what fun! . . .

Tyltyl. They're getting the cakes! . . . They can touch them! . . . They're eating, they're eating, they're eating! . . .

Mytyl. The tiny ones, too! . . . They've got two, three, four apiece! . . .

Tyltyl (*drunk with delight*). Oh, how lovely! . . . Oh, how lovely, how lovely! . . .

Mytyl (*counting imaginary cakes*). I've got twelve! . . .

Tyltyl. And I four times twelve! . . . But I'll give you some. . . .

[*A knock at the door of the cottage.*]

Tyltyl (*suddenly quieted and frightened*). What's that? . . .

Mytyl (*scared*). It's Daddy! . . .

[*As they hesitate before opening the door, the big latch is seen to rise of itself.*]

"You're being Petrova," Doctor Jakes would say, "who has just eaten a good breakfast, not Mytyl who never has quite enough to eat, watching other children having more cakes than she has ever seen. 'The tiny ones too! . . . They've got two, three, four apiece!' . . . Come on, you're Mytyl, pleased that other children shall have cakes, but absolutely amazed that any child can be lucky enough to have four at once."

To help her Doctor Jakes and Doctor Smith called her Mytyl always at lessons, and arranged for Sylvia to call her Mytyl at meals; Pauline, of course, was Tyltyl; but not like the boy in the play, for she did not do most of the talking, but said things to make Mytyl talk. Geography, History, Arithmetic—it was all the same. Petrova was the child of poor simple people, pleased to think of the wonderful books other children had, and how clever other people were, but not expecting anything much herself. Of course it was easy at meals, because they were rather like the play.

In spite of all the trouble taken by everybody, there were lots of days when she nearly had the part taken away from her. It was she herself who suggested something which made rehearsing much easier. They were doing the very difficult scene in the churchyard:

> [*It is night. The moon is shining on a country graveyard. Numerous tomb-*

*stones, grassy mounds, wooden crosses,
stone slabs, etc.* TYLTYL *and* MYTYL *are
standing by a short stone pillar.*]

Mytyl.   I am frightened! . . .

Tyltyl (not too much at his ease). I am never frightened. . . .

Mytyl.   I say, are the dead wicked? . . .

Tyltyl.   Why, no, they're not alive! . . .

Mytyl.   Have you ever seen one? . . .

Tyltyl.   Yes, once, long ago, when I was very young. . . .

Mytyl.   What was it like, say? . . .

Tyltyl.   Quite white, very still and very cold, and it didn't talk. . . .

Mytyl.   Are we going to see them, say? . . .

Tyltyl.   Why, of course, Light said so. . . .

Mytyl.   Where are they? . . .

Tyltyl.   Here, under the grass or under those big stones. . . .

Mytyl.   Are they there all the year round? . . .

Tyltyl.   Yes.

Mytyl (pointing to the slabs). Are those the doors of their houses? . . .

Tyltyl.   Yes.

Mytyl.   Do they go out when it's fine? . . .

Tyltyl.   They can only go out at night. . . .

Mytyl. Why?

Tyltyl. Because they are in their shirts. . . .

Mytyl. Do they go out also when it rains? . . .

Tyltyl. When it rains they stay at home. . . .

Mytyl. Is it nice in their homes, say? . . .

Tyltyl. They say it's very cramped. . . .

Mytyl. Have they any little children? . . .

Tyltyl. Why, yes; they have all those that die. . . .

Mytyl. And what do they live on? . . .

Tyltyl. They eat roots. . . .

Mytyl. Shall we see them? . . .

Tyltyl. Of course; we see everything when I turn the diamond.

Mytyl. And what will they say? . . .

Tyltyl. They will say nothing, as they don't talk. . . .

Mytyl. Why don't they talk? . . .

Tyltyl. Because they have nothing to say. . . .

Mytyl. Why have they nothing to say? . . .

Tyltyl. You're a nuisance. . . .

        [A pause.]

Mytyl. When will you turn the diamond?

Tyltyl. You heard Light say that I was to wait until midnight, because that disturbs them less. . . .

Mytyl. Why does that disturb them less? . . .

Tyltyl. Because that is when they go out to take the air. . . .

Mytyl. Is it not midnight yet? . . .

Tyltyl. Do you see the church clock? . . .

Mytyl. Yes, I can even see the small hand. . . .

Tyltyl. Well, midnight is just going to strike. . . . There! . . . Do you hear? . . .

[*The clock strikes twelve.*]

Mytyl. I want to go away! . . .

Tyltyl. Not now. . . . I am going to turn the diamond. . . .

Mytyl. No, No! . . . Don't . . . I want to go away! . . . I am so frightened, little brother! . . . I am terribly frightened! . . .

Tyltyl. But there is no danger. . . .

Mytyl. I don't want to see the dead! . . . I don't want to see them! . . .

Tyltyl. Very well, you shall not see them; shut your eyes. . . .

Mytyl (*clinging to* TYLTYL's *clothes*). Tyltyl, I can't stay! . . . No, I can't possibly! . . . They are going to come out of the ground! . . .

Tyltyl. Don't tremble like that. . . . They will only come out for a moment. . . .

Mytyl. But you're trembling too! . . . They will be awful! . . .

Tyltyl. It is time, the hour is passing. . . .

[TYLTYL *turns the diamond.*]

Petrova could not be frightened enough. Miss Jay stopped the rehearsal over and over again.

"Petrova, dear, remember you are frightened. You are in a churchyard alone with your little brother in the middle of the night, and you know that in a minute or two he is going to turn the diamond on his cap which you think will bring all the ghosts out of their graves. You are cold and shivering. . . ." She stopped because Petrova was crying. She put her arm round her. "Don't cry because you can't act, my child; save those tears up for when you are acting. If you could cry like that when you say: 'I want to go away! . . . I am so frightened, little brother!' then we should get something from you; now we get nothing except Petrova saying lines that she has learned."

Petrova went on sobbing.

"I don't feel like Mytyl," she choked, "just standing here in uniform looking exactly like Pauline. I don't even feel she's my brother; it doesn't feel like night; if only I was dressed up. . . ."

After that the children were dressed for every rehearsal. They did not wear the actual clothes they would wear at the matinée, of course; but Pauline wore shorts and a shirt, and Petrova an apron and a red-riding-hood cloak over her frock. The clothes made a great difference: as soon as they were put on they

were Tyltyl and Mytyl, and though Petrova was still
often made to say a sentence ten or twenty times over
at each rehearsal, people stopped wondering if she was
good enough to play the part.

In the dancing classes the same strenuous work was
going on. Even children as small and smaller than
Posy were expected to rehearse thirteen hours a week,
as well as doing their ordinary lessons. Posy had nothing to say, but she danced as an Hour, and a Star, and
she was an unborn child. To her the dancing rehearsals
were easy; but they caused a lot of tears among the
other children. They were never allowed to forget that
they were training for the professional stage, and slov-
enly work was therefore inexcusable. The dances, once
learned, had to be performed as to timing, entrance,
and sequence of steps. Any child who, after reasonable
rehearsal, made a mistake was turned out, and no arguing was allowed; sobs and pleading fell on deaf ears.
Even Posy had to concentrate so hard that she usually
slept all the way home. Sometimes Petrova and Pauline
did, too, but they were rather ashamed when they did.
There was some excuse, they thought, for Posy, who
would not be eight until September, but none at all
for themselves.

Over the making of the clothes Mrs. Simpson,
Cook, and Clara helped Nana. Each child had three

changes. Tyltyl and Mytyl had only night things
when the curtain rose; but they then changed into
very plain peasant dress, and from that into their grand
fairy-tale frocks. Pauline, as Hop O' My Thumb, had
scarlet satin knickers and a pale blue satin coat, and
Petrova a Red Riding Hood dress—a jade-green satin
frock and a black-velvet bodice and white blouse and
apron under her scarlet cloak. Posy's dresses were only
little bits of chiffon; but they took time, and time
was a thing there was very little of in that house. Even
fittings for the dresses had to be squeezed out of time
that belonged to walks or meals.

One day at the beginning of July, when the children really had stopped making mistakes at rehearsals,
and were so tired of the play that they wished that it had
never been written, and so tired from hard work that
they thought everybody else was being horrid to them,
they went down on to the tube station at Gloucester
Road, and there saw the first poster about the matinée.
At the top it said all about the hospital, and under
that, very large, "Matinée of The Blue Bird," and
under that, "By Maurice Maeterlinck"; then under
that, in small letters, "Performed by the students of
. . ."; then in large letters "The Children's Academy
of Dancing and Stage Training"; then followed a list
of all the famous ex-students who were dancing and

acting. Right at the bottom was written "Tyltyl . . .
Pauline Fossil"; "Mytyl . . . Petrova Fossil".

Nana and the three children stared at the poster,
reading every word from top to bottom. When they
got into the train, Posy expressed the pride that they
all felt.

"To think that we should have our name stuck up
in a train!"

VIII

The Matinée

*

ON THE DAY of the matinée Pauline woke very early, but Petrova was awake before her. Petrova was sitting up in bed with both her hands holding that bit that comes in the middle just below the bottom ribs.

"What are you doing?" Pauline asked.

Petrova did not move her hands.

"This bit of me feels very queer—like when you miss a step on the moving staircase and think you are going to fall to the bottom."

Pauline shook herself. Then she held the same place.

"That bit of me feels the same. Do you think it's the matinée this afternoon?"

"Yes." Petrova's voice wobbled with fright. "I'm afraid I'll forget my words."

"Even if you did, Miss Jay is standing in the prompt corner with the book, and she says if we look at her she will tell us what to say."

"I know." Petrova sounded very depressed. "But all the same I do, *do* wish it was over."

Pauline thought a moment, and thinking of the afternoon, her inside felt most extraordinary.

"Oh, so do I," she agreed with fervor.

Nana came in, and found them both holding their middles.

"What's that for?" she asked, drawing up the blind.

"Our insides feel queer because of this afternoon," Pauline explained.

"Stuff and nonsense," said Nana. "Your insides feel queer because they want breakfast. With the lovely performance you all gave at the dress rehearsal, there's nothing to feel queer about." She sat down between them. "How would those insides feel if they had breakfast in bed, with sausages?"

Breakfast in bed only happened when they were ill, and sausages only on Sundays, so one way and another their insides felt a lot steadier, even before Nana brought in the trays. Just as they were going to eat, Posy came in with nothing on but the bath-mat and gave an imitation of the ex-student who was being "Water" at the matinée. "Water" was a very good dancer, but she had rather a big behind, and in Posy's imitation it did not look any smaller; and they all laughed so much that Nana made Posy stop because she thought they would upset their tea into their beds.

No inside could feel even a bit queer after laughing like that.

When they were dressed, Pauline got them all into a corner. It was, she said, a very important day, seeing that their name was going to be printed on programs for the first time, and she thought they ought to vow.

Posy looked shocked.

"But it's nobody's birthday."

"Doesn't have to be," Pauline argued. "We said we'd always vow on a birthday, but we never said we wouldn't vow on other days." She started quickly:

"We three Fossils vow to try and put our name into History books because it's our very own and nobody can say it's because of our Grandfathers."

"We vow," said Petrova and Posy, and held up their hands.

Posy, who was feeling silly because she was excited, did what she had not done since the first vowing: she spoke deep in her inside, which she could not do, and a most extraordinary sound came out. For a moment Pauline and Petrova looked cross, then suddenly they began to laugh, and they laughed so long that Nana came in.

"There's no need to act silly because you're doing a matinée," she said, but she did not look cross.

Then she told them that Cook wanted Pauline to

come and help her ice some cakes, and that Mr. Simpson said would Petrova come and help in the garage, and that he was waiting for her in the car, and Posy was to go and put her things on, as she was to help do some very special shopping.

Cook was in her nicest mood. She let Pauline do all the icing on the cakes, which were for late tea when they all got back from the matinée, and let her squeeze names and patterns on them. She enjoyed herself so much and was so busy that she forgot all about the afternoon, and was amazed when Nana said it was time to wash for their lunch, which was to be at half-past twelve.

Petrova enjoyed her drive to the garage less than usual. Away from Pauline the feeling in her front came back. She had to hold it again, and told Mr. Simpson about it. He understood at once; he said he often had just that feeling himself; he especially remembered it when he had to go and stop a native strike. He had not been quite sure how things would turn out, and his inside had felt most peculiar. He had found then, he said, whistling had been a help. Petrova explained that she could not whistle, so he said, How about singing then? He started with "Three Blind Mice," and she joined in, and then he went on to "Where Are You Going To," followed by "There's a Long, Long

Trail" and "Daisy, Daisy". By that time they were in Piccadilly, and people stared at them, but he did not mind.

"If anybody asks us why we are singing," he said, "we'll say we are the S.F.S. league, The Stop, Front, Swellers."

Inside the garage he had a surprise for her. She usually put a mackintosh on to keep herself clean; but today he gave her a parcel, and inside was a suit of jeans, just like garage men wear, only, of course, her size. He sent her behind the door to change, and when she came out she felt so pleased with herself looking so like a real mechanic that she forgot all about the matinée, and settled down at once to cleaning a car, and she was just as surprised as Pauline when she heard it was time to go home to lunch.

Posy and Nana went to a shop, and Nana fetched some little boxes. Posy wanted to know what was in them, but Nana would not say. Posy was not feeling at all worried about the afternoon; she knew she would enjoy it because it was dancing, and she did not care a bit if there was an audience or not.

Lunch would have been difficult to eat because they were all so excited; but there was cold chicken and jelly, both of which are easy to eat whatever you feel like.

Mr. Simpson drove them to the theater. Inside the stage door the doorkeeper stopped them and asked their names, and then with a smile he looked in a shelf which was alphabetically numbered, and out of a pigeon-hole marked F took a whole lot of telegrams. There were four each for Petrova and Pauline, and two for Posy. They each had one from the Simpsons, and one from the two doctors, and Pauline and Petrova's other two came from Madame, and from somebody signing herself "Olga". It said in Pauline's "Good luck, Tyltyl", and in Petrova's "Good luck, Mytyl". For a moment nobody could remember who Olga was, and then they remembered she was the Russian child the hospital had nursed, who was now a nurse in the hospital. They were all very impressed at her sending telegrams.

Pauline and Petrova had a room to themselves, but Posy came and dressed there too, because it saved trouble. In the fun of getting dressed and Theo coming to make them up, they had not time even to think if they were frightened or not, until suddenly there was a knock on the door and the voice of the call-boy said: "Quarter of an hour. Please."

"Does that mean that we start in a quarter of an hour?" Pauline asked Theo in a wavering voice.

She nodded and laughed; but neither Pauline nor

Petrova saw anything to laugh at. They sat down side by side feeling scared stiff. It seemed a very short time after that when the call-boy came again, this time to say, "Overture and beginners. Please."

Theo took them each by the hand, and they went down the stairs and through the swing doors on to the stage. There she kissed them, and then they went on to the stage, and got into bed, where Miss Jay tucked them in, and gave them a pat and told them not to be frightened. The orchestra seemed to go on playing the overture for a very long time, then suddenly the house lights were out, the curtain was going up.

For her first three sentences Pauline was not sure what her voice was doing. It seemed to squeak in an odd way. Her third sentence, "No; how can I be asleep when I'm talking to you?" made the audience laugh. It was a nice friendly laugh, as though all the people in the audience were like Mr. and Mrs. Simpson, and from that moment she began to enjoy herself, and to have a sure feeling that the audience were enjoying themselves too.

Petrova's mouth felt dry; she could hear in her head just how each word ought to sound, and yet it did not come out quite right. She heard the laugh when Pauline said: "How can I be asleep when I'm talking to you?" and she remembered clearly all she had been taught about laughs. Wait for it. Never speak while the audience are laughing. Speak as the laugh dies away. She had rehearsed laughs with a phonograph; but now here was a real one, and she was not quite sure when to speak, and when she did, she knew it was too soon, and nobody had heard what she said. They came to the part where she and Tyltyl had to quarrel over the stool and she was pushed off and said: "I'm looking at the wall because I've got no room," and the audience laughed again. At once she felt better, her mouth got less dry, and she did not worry about what came next; and though still some of the lines did not sound much like Mytyl, but more like Petrova, she had stopped minding.

When the curtain came down on the act, everybody seemed pleased, and Pauline and Petrova went back to their dressing-room and did not feel miserable any more, and instead played about giving imitations of each other, while Posy gave imitations of the dancers until Nana lost her temper.

"Will you sit down and behave like little ladies. What the other children must be thinking with all this noise, I don't know."

Pauline giggled.

"But we aren't little ladies. Petrova and I are poor children of a woodcutter, and Posy's a star."

"Whatever you are, you'll behave," Nana said firmly, "or I'll fetch Miss Jay. She said you were to rest."

The mention of fetching Miss Jay calmed them down, and they sat quiet till they were called for the next act.

It was odd that the scene which Petrova most hated she acted better than any other that afternoon. It was the scene in the churchyard that had given her so much trouble. Somehow when she and Pauline were left alone on the stage, it all looked so dark and the gravestones so real that she almost made herself believe that ghosts would come when the diamond was turned; and therefore when it was turned, and there were nothing but lilies to be seen, she was honestly quite surprised, and said in the most natural way, "Where are the dead?" . . . and was glad to hear Pauline reply, "There are no dead". . . .

The play was over, all the cast stood on the stage and bowed, with Pauline and Petrova standing alone in the front. Then Madame came on. Pauline and Petrova wondered if they ought to curtsy, and looked round to make sure, but none of the others did, so they supposed it was all right not to. Madame spoke to the audience. She said they had just heard Tyltyl ask if

any of them should find his bluebird to give it back
as: "We need it for our happiness later on".

"Today you have helped a hospital, whose bluebird
has flown away because of financial worry. With sub-
scriptions and the tickets this afternoon we have a thousand pounds for them, which we hope will help to
bring their bluebird back for their 'happiness later
on' ".

A thousand pounds was such a lot of money that
everybody cheered, and somebody from the hospital
made a speech from a box, then "God Save the King"
was played, and the matinée was over.

When they got home there was a most magnificent
tea waiting. Everybody in the house had been to the
matinée, and they all had something to say about it.
Cook, that it had given her a good cry, which was
high praise, as she liked crying. Clara said it was better than the pictures, which was higher praise still.
Doctor Jakes was very nice, and said they had worked
very well and deserved their success. She was even
nicer to Petrova than to Pauline.

"You did very well, my dear," she said. "It's easy
for Pauline, but it's anything but easy for you."

"Sorry it's over?" Mr. Simpson asked them all.

Pauline said she was very, Posy was rather, and
Petrova suddenly found she was glad; this afternoon

had been fun, but it was nice to think there'd be no more of those awful rehearsals.

Tea was finished, and they were still talking about the afternoon when suddenly Pauline burst into tears. Pauline was not a person who ever cried, so everybody was surprised, except Doctor Jakes, who said it was quite a natural thing to do. Sylvia hugged her.

"What is it, darling?"

"Everything's over," Pauline sniffed, "and nothing nice will ever happen again."

"That's talking stupidly, Pauline," said Nana. "Just take a look at your plate."

While Pauline had been crying, Nana had put the little boxes she and Posy had fetched that morning on their plates. There was great excitement, and when they were opened there was a brooch in each from Sylvia with a little enamel bluebird on it. On the back of each bird were their names and the date. After they had thanked for them, and pinned them on to their frocks, Sylvia told them she had news for them. They had all worked so hard that she had rented a tiny cottage at Pevensey Bay, in Sussex, and they were going there for August.

After that, of course, Pauline could not feel that nothing nice would ever happen again. Petrova thought a cottage in Sussex nicer than any matinée. It was Posy, though, who sent them all to bed laughing. She slipped down again after her bath, and poked her head round the door, and looked solemnly at Pauline, whose face was still a bit blotchy from having cried, and quoted a line from "The Blue Bird":

"And Pauline has still got a pimple on her nose."

IX

Pauline Wants a New Frock

*

THEY had a lovely time at Pevensey. There was very little money to spend, but except for eating, they did not need any. They came down to the beach in their bathing-dresses early in the morning and spent all day there. They found a smooth piece of fine shingle where nobody could see them and did exercises for half an hour in the morning; after tea they worked on the small bit of lawn at the back of the cottage, as there was a fence round it just the right height to make a good practice bar. They had lots of walks to the old castle, and once they went to Eastbourne and had tea on Beachy Head. They got very brown, and all put on weight, and ate more every day.

The Cromwell Road seemed very long and dull when they got back; but they had not time to think much about it, for term at the Academy began the next day.

That Autumn term was like the last Autumn term; by the end of it those children who were not old enough for a license felt out of things, for everybody else was rehearsing for Christmas productions. Pauline hated it. She had been so important all last term, and now she was rather in the way. She was in a class older than her age, and so was left with nobody to work with. It was a continual "Pauline, dear, sit quietly down and watch". She loathed it; she loathed to be made to feel not wanted when she knew she was the best actress in the class. So she sulked. It was not her fault that she was not twelve; she would be next year, thank goodness! and in the meantime she would not be nice and helpful, and run round fetching and carrying for other people's rehearsals; she would go on coming to the class, but be as much in the way as possible. She thought nobody was noticing how she felt, but she was wrong. One day about three weeks before the end of the term she came to the class as usual, but was stopped in the doorway by Miss Jay.

"I shan't want you again this term, Pauline, I am too busy working on the Christmas plays. You will go to Madame Moulin instead."

Pauline usually had two French acting classes a week and found them quite enough, for learning a part in French was not as easy to her as learning it in English. Madame Moulin greeted her with a cheerful nod when she saw her.

"Ah, *ma petite,* next term I will have you play the

'Little Match-girl' of Hans Andersen. I translate myself in the holidays; but now, since I have you for five extra hours a week, I shall give it to you; you shall start the translating for me."

Pauline's mouth dropped open. She stared at Madame Moulin in horror.

"But that isn't acting, that's lessons. I hate doing translations."

"It's very good for you." Madame patted her shoulder. "Miss Jay had thought it would be amusing for you to watch the senior girls prepare for the Christmas plays, the extra rehearsals that she takes so that they may please their producers; but she tells me, 'No, Pauline *ne s'amuse pas;* she knows too much of the art of acting to be interested in the training of these others. We must find her something difficult to do— it is bad for a child to be bored'." She pulled out a chair, and pointed to the sheets of foolscap, and a copy of Hans Andersen's fairy story. "There you are, *ma chère*. You will not have time to be bored if you translate all this for a play."

Pauline had to sit down. Angrily she took up the book, and began to read the story. Madame Moulin settled at the other end of the room and took a pencil and cut lines out of a play that the junior class were to be given. Pauline tried to read, but she had a lump in her throat, and though she meant not to cry, tears came into her eyes and the words kept getting blurred; then quite suddenly from trying not to cry a sob came out that was like a hiccup. That started her. She could not stop; it seemed so mean that she should be treated like this. The more she thought how mean it was, the more she cried. Madame said after a bit:

"Why are you crying?"

Pauline brought out a long sentence, but none of it was distinguishable. It sounded like: "Mean-hateful-French-mean-why?-Not-done-anything-mean-it's mean-snotsmifaultwelve".

Madame looked out of the window, and thought a moment.

"When I was a young girl I was a pupil of the Académie Française. I was a good pupil; I had great promise, just as you have great promise. I grew, as many young girls grow, to think I had more than promise. One day there came to the school a very great actress. She was old, and one of her legs had been cut off, so she used one of wood. It chanced that I had recently had much notice for my playing of 'L'Aiglon'."

Pauline was crying less, because she was interested.

" 'L'Aiglon?' That's an eagle, isn't it?"

"Yes. A poor young boy, he was the eaglet; you

shall read the story, and when you are fifteen or sixteen you could play it. This actress, she was a very old woman and she chose that role to act for the students. Imagine her! Old. A wooden leg. Dressed in the height of fashion. To play a young boy!"

"How silly!" said Pauline.

"That is what I thought." Madame Moulin nodded. "How foolish! *C'est formidable!* That old woman 'L'Aiglon'! I am 'L'Aiglon'; I am young, but I settled to watch, saying, 'Well, we must be kind, but . . .' Pauline, when she had finished, the tears ran down my cheeks. She was 'L'Aiglon'. She ceased to be ridiculous, her art was supreme. How we students clapped! How we called *'Bis'*. When we were dismissed, we passed her bowing; but when I drew level with her she caught my hand. It was as though she had read in my face how I had thought, for she said, *'N'oubliez jamais qu'une actrice continue à apprendre jusqu'à son dernier jour'*." Pauline looked a little puzzled, so she translated: "Never forget that an actress can always learn until her last hour."

"I want to learn," Pauline said sulkily. "It's because I wasn't learning that I didn't like it; and anyway I never said so."

"Your face said it, and Miss Jay could see. You were angry. Why should you watch these girls? What

had they to teach you? You, who had played Tyltyl
so well. You were in the mood I was in when I watched
'L'Aiglon'. Why should I watch? What could an old
woman teach me?"

"But you were watching a great actress."

"It never matters whom you watch, you can always
learn. Always, always, always. Now bring your book
here. Together we will translate the story. At the end
of next term we will give a performance of it, in cos-
tume."

Posy came to her class and was told that Madame
could not take her as she had to coach a girl for a pantomime; she was to go to a general class. This happened three days running; then Posy took the law into
her own hands. She paid no attention to the message,
and went on upstairs just as though she had not re-
ceived it. She knocked on Madame's door and went in
and curtsied. Madame was giving a lesson; she looked
round with a frown.

"What is it, Posy dear?"

"I've come to say good-bye," said Posy cheerfully. "I'm not coming any more this term except for
fencing."

"Why?"

"The class I'm going to isn't any good to me."

Madame's eyes grew very small, and looked angry; she hated disobedience.

"I have arranged for you to attend it."

"Yes." Posy smiled at her happily. "But you don't know what they do." She came over to the bar. "Those frappés are over too quick: no time to get them right. Then there are two exercises you and I don't do, and I won't do them until you've shown me. Not any of it does me good, so I'll work at home just like you've showed me, and I'll come again next term."

Madame looked for a moment as though she would hit her. Then suddenly she laughed.

"How old are you?"

"Eight."

Madame kissed her.

"Good-bye. If you don't come to classes I rely on your honor to work at home, and all through the holidays. I shall take you for extra classes next term."

The pantomime rehearsals suited Petrova. Some of the children in her class were dancing in troupes, and nobody had time for those that were not. They were supposed to work at the bar by themselves; but of course they never did, but had a glorious time doing anything they liked.

The next year was an important year. Pauline would be twelve at the beginning of December, and so old enough to have a license, and they all had whooping-cough.

Whooping-cough is a miserable disease, but if you must have it, the worst place is the Cromwell Road; it is so far from the Parks and any place where you can whoop nicely in private. They spent the first part of having it in bed, but after a bit they got well enough to get up, and then it was most depressing. The weather was ghastly—very cold, with the sort of winds which cut your legs and face, and often it rained and sometimes half snowed. They whooped too much to go on an underground, or a bus; they were all cross, and they got more and more tired of walking to the Victoria and Albert and back. Then one day Mrs. Simpson remembered that an old housemaid they had when she was a girl lived in the country and was poor, and would be glad to have them. Sylvia was worried, because what money she had was getting steadily less, and there was not a word from Gum. But Mrs. Simpson said it would not cost much, and that it would be a present to the children from her because the garage was doing well, and she thought it was because, as a family, they had brought them luck.

The cottage was in the middle of a common in

Kent. It was a perfect place for whooping-cough, because there never was anybody about, and if there chanced to be a passer-by and a whoop came on, there were plenty of gorse-bushes. As a matter of fact, directly they got there they began to whoop less. The weather got better, and they found early primroses, and the catkins and pussy palm showed there would not be much more winter, and at once they felt better. Nana, who was fussy about gloves and looking like ladies even when you were going to look anything but a lady and stand whooping in the road, seemed to change in the country. She was country born herself, and she so liked helping Gladys (the housemaid Mrs. Simpson had when she was a girl) with the chickens, and putting up Gladys's husband's dinner, which meant popping a bit of bacon into a pastry turnover, and looking over the potatoes in the barn, that she never bothered the children at all. As long as they were out all day, and ate plenty, she did not even get angry when they came in late for meals. They went back to London without a whoop in them in time for the Summer term.

That Summer term and the beginning of the Autumn were very hard working for Pauline. She would be twelve in December. A child can get a license to

act from her twelfth birthday. Pauline was to try and
get her first engagement that Christmas.

"Pauline," said Miss Jay one day in November.
"I want you here at eleven tomorrow morning. I want
you to bring a length of hair-ribbon with you and to
wear a nice frock. I am taking you to see a manager."

The news that Pauline was to see a manager the
next day caused more confusion than pleasure. Gum's
money was getting lower and lower; and since eating
is the most important thing, everybody had to do
without new clothes. Nana did miracles in the way of
patching and darning, but of course patches and darns,
though neat, are not smart. The only dresses the children had that could be described as "nice" in the way
in which Miss Jay meant, were their white organdies,
and Pauline could not wear white organdie with a blue
sash at eleven o'clock on a November morning. For
lessons, and to go to the Academy, they had kilted
skirts, and jerseys, and on Sundays and better occa-
sions they still had velvet frocks which Sylvia had
bought them when times were not so bad; but Pauline's was much too short for her now, and one of the
elbows was darned. Nana took it out of the cupboard
and held it up to the light.

"Terrible!" She shook her head. "Nobody'd engage you for anything, Pauline, looking like a rag-bag

in that. I'll just wash your jersey through tonight, and you'll have to wear what you've got on."

Pauline got very red.

"I can't. Miss Jay will think we haven't any clothes if I wear a jersey and skirt after her saying a frock."

"Well you haven't any, so there's no harm in her thinking it." Nana spoke crossly, because she hated the children not to be well dressed.

The three children looked at each other. They knew all about going to auditions for parts, for they had seen it happen. You came to school in best clothes, and stood in the hall where everybody could see you, and people called out "Good luck! I hope you get it."

"She can't go in a jersey and skirt, Nana," Petrova said.

"No." Posy looked very determined. "Jerseys and skirts are never worn at auditions."

"Well"—Nana sounded crosser than ever, but they all knew she was not—"what do you think I am? A conjurer? Do you think I can make a frock like they bring rabbits out of a hat?"

In the ordinary way they would have laughed at that, but they did not now. Going to an audition in old clothes was far too serious a matter. They could hear the whispers, and see the nudges, "Those Fossils haven't any clothes."

Petrova clenched her hands.

"They're not going to be sorry for us—they shan't. Pauline has got to have a frock."

"If only we had some money." Pauline went over to the velvet dress. "Do you suppose I'll have to take my coat off? The front isn't so awful."

They all examined the frock. It had that going-different-ways look that velvet gets when it is old. It had been a nice blue once, but it was grayish in parts now; the darn on the elbow showed terribly, and so did the place where the hem had been let down. After a moment they left the frock. There was no need to say anything: it was obvious she could not wear it.

"Do you think Garnie has a little money?" Posy suggested.

Pauline and Petrova answered together.

"We can't tell her, she mustn't know."

"No," Nana agreed, thinking of all the extra gray hairs in Sylvia's head, and the hours she spent working out accounts, and knowing how badly, even with the boarders' money, they worked out. "We mustn't bother Miss Brown."

"I know!" Petrova exclaimed. "Our necklaces! They'd sell."

"Oh!" Posy let out the gasp before she had time to hold it back, because she was very fond of her corals.

Then she took a deep breath and said in as pleased a voice as she could, "Our necklaces! What a good idea!"

"There's our watches," Pauline said. "Wouldn't they do instead? I'd rather sell my watch."

"No." Petrova looked at her watch. "We always wear those. Garnie would be sure to ask where they were."

Pauline looked worried.

"Well, couldn't we just sell my necklace?"

Nana shook her head.

"Turquoises don't fetch much, dear."

"But pearls do," Petrova said. "Perhaps just mine would do."

"But it's for a frock for me," Pauline protested.

Petrova sat on the floor to think better.

"It's for us all really. It would be all our shame if you had to go in a jersey and skirt."

"Tell you what," Nana suggested. "Let's take all three necklaces along, and see what is offered. We couldn't get a dress in a hurry for Pauline under four or five guineas. It's no good buying cheap stuff, it's got to last."

"I tell you what." Pauline sat down by Petrova. "Suppose we buy a dress with our necklaces and keep it for nothing but auditions. Let's get one that'll suit all of us."

"Doesn't matter awfully about it suiting me," Posy pointed out. "I can't go to an audition for nearly four years."

"Unless the Professor's back," Nana said in a voice which showed what she thought of the Professor, "it's what you'll wear for more than four years."

"Very awkward it's going to be," Petrova observed, "when all of us are old enough for licenses and want to wear it on the same day."

Pauline looked proud.

"You seem to forget that I'm going to an audition about a part. If I get it I shall earn money. Probably by the time Posy is twelve I shall be keeping you all."

Posy put on an American twang.

"And how!"

The plan was that Pauline and Nana should go out as soon as the shops were open, taking the three neck-laces with them. All their plans were upset, however, by Mr. Simpson coming up after breakfast just as they were starting, and saying that since it was a most im-portant occasion he intended to drive Pauline to the Academy. Pauline looked at the others, and none of them knew what to say. Then Posy blurted out:

"But you can't. She's got to . . ."

Petrova put her hand over her mouth and stopped her saying any more; but of course Mr. Simpson could not help seeing something was odd.

He looked at them, then he sat down and asked Nana if he might light his pipe. Nana said he could, and while he was seeing to it they made signs to each other to say he must not be told anything. When his pipe was going nicely he looked round and smiled.

"What's the trouble, Nana?"

"Nothing, sir," Nana said firmly.

He sighed.

"Oh, dear, I hoped I was a really trusted friend, but I suppose I'm not." He got up. "Very well, then, I'll go to the garage if I can't help with a lift, Pauline."

Pauline and Petrova looked at each other in a worried way. They felt awful, and Petrova made a face at Pauline to say "Couldn't we tell him?" Then suddenly Nana said:

"If you wouldn't mind stepping outside a minute, sir."

He went at once, and then she told them that she thought they had better tell him, for gentlemen knew about jewelry, and perhaps he would not only drive them to a shop where they could sell the necklaces, but see the man in the shop did not cheat them. Nana thought everybody cheated women, and had great faith in a man being about. So they called Mr. Simpson in and told him the whole story. He listened, then he said he had a better scheme. He got out a piece of paper and a fountain pen. He wrote a lot. Then he spoke like a man at a board meeting.

"I will advance you five pounds on those necklaces: at the rate of thirty shillings each for Pauline's and Posy's and two pounds for Petrova's because pearls are more expensive. Pauline will buy them back week by week out of the money she earns. First Posy's, because the frock is likely to be least use to her, then Petrova's, and last, her own. If Pauline hasn't managed to buy them back by the time Petrova's working, then Petrova will help, and the same applies to you, Posy. Now, as Miss Brown will certainly worry if she knew you had to sell the necklaces to get a frock, Nana will come down and borrow them on any occasion when you usually wear them. If this arrangement suits you, will you please all three sign? And Nana must sign as witness."

The children said nothing for a moment because it seemed such an easy plan, but sounded so business-like. Then Petrova asked:

"If we don't earn money quickly to buy them back, will you sell them to get your five pounds?"

I John Simpson, agree to purchase Great Uncle Matthew's necklaces for five pounds: Pauline to buy the said necklaces back out of her earnings at the rate of thirty shillings each for Pauline's & Posy's and two pounds for Petrova's. Should Pauline not have completed the purchase by the time Petrova is working she will assist in the repayments, this also applies to Posy

Signed
Pauline Fossil.
Petrova Fossil.
Posy Fossil.

Witnessed by Alice Gutheridge Nov. 8th 1931.
(Nana)

Mr. Simpson nodded.

"Naturally, but since we are friends I will keep them as long as I can." He laid the piece of paper on the table and held out his pen. "You first, Pauline. Sign here."

X

The Audition

*

THERE is no doubt a new dress is a help under all circumstances. This new one was very becoming to Pauline, whose hair had got no darker as she grew older, but had remained a natural platinum. All the children considered velvet the right material for an audition frock, and in Harrods, Nana and Pauline found a black chiffon velvet dress. It was plainly made, with a white collar and white cuffs, and a tight bodice with rows of buttons down the back. Pauline wished it was not black, which she thought dull, and like their elocution overalls; but it was the right sort of thing to wear, and had the advantage that there was an enormous hem to let down, and that the black knickers that belonged to her overall would do to wear under it. Mr. Simpson waited outside Harrods in the car, and though it was too cold to take her coat off, Pauline unbuttoned it so that he could see what the money he had lent had bought. He said she looked magnificent, and all the way to the Academy he pretended he was driving a debutante to a Court at Buckingham Palace.

Pauline left her hat in the cloakroom, and she and Nana went and stood in the hall. Nana carried her coat, for the students were always inspected before they went to an audition. There was one other child waiting, who had her mother with her. Her name was Winifred and she was very clever. She was the child who would have played Mytyl if she had not had measles. She acted really well, she was a brilliant dancer, she had an unusually good singing voice, but she was not pretty. She had a clever, interesting face, and long, but rather colorless, brown hair. She was wearing an ugly brown velvet frock; not a good choice of color, as it made her look the same all over. When Winifred's mother saw Nana, she gave her Winifred's coat and shoe bag and hair-ribbon, and asked her to be so kind as to look after her, as she could not well spare a morning; her husband was ill, and there were five children younger than Winifred at home.

Winifred looked enviously at Pauline.

"What a lovely frock! I can hardly breathe in mine, it's so tight. I bought it last year out of the money I made in Pantomime. I've grown since."

Pauline flushed. It was not her secret how she had got the money for the dress, so she could not explain; but she did not want Winifred to think she often had things like that.

"I borrowed the money for mine," she whispered. "But don't tell the others."

Winifred nodded to show she would not.

"We're going for 'Alice,' " she said.

" 'In Wonderland'?" asked Pauline. "How do you know?"

Winifred held out the hair-ribbon which she was holding.

"Whenever they put on 'Alice in Wonderland' and they are taking people down about 'Alice', they tell them to bring hair-ribbons. I should think you might get it. I wish I would, though."

"It would be lovely!" Pauline's eyes shone at the thought. "Fancy meeting all the people, the Frog Footman, and the Mad Hatter, and . . ."

"And think of the money!" Winifred added.

Pauline thought of the necklaces.

"Would one earn much?"

Winifred looked wise.

"It's the Princess Theater; it's a mean management. Ought to get six, but it'll be more likely four . . . they might squeeze five."

"Five what?" asked Pauline. "Shillings?"

Winifred stared at her.

"Shillings! Pounds. Don't you need money at home?"

Pauline thought of Gum, and Sylvia's gray hairs, and the boarders.

"Of course."

Winifred pulled up her socks.

"There's needing money, and needing money," she said wisely. "If I could get this job, Mother'd put half away for me, but even what's left would mean the extra stuff Dad needs to get well. He's had an operation, and doesn't seem to get right after it. Then there's clothes wanted for all of us, especially shoes. Oh, it would be wonderful if I could get it!"

She looked so anxious that Pauline almost hoped she would. Of course she needed the money too, but somehow, although there was not any for new clothes, and the food was getting plainer and plainer, nobody had ever said what a help it would be when she could earn some, and certainly she had never worried about it as poor Winifred seemed to do. All the time Winifred was talking people who walked by called out, "Good luck, Winifred, good luck, Pauline." Pauline could see from the way they looked at her that they thought she looked nice, and from the way they looked at Winifred, that they thought she did not. She wished she had some money and could buy Winifred a new frock; she was so nice and she looked so all-wrong.

When Miss Jay came, she turned both Winifred

and Pauline round and said, "Very nice," and though it was impossible that she thought Winifred looked nice in her mustardy-brown frock, which was too small for her, there was nothing in her voice to show it. She told them both that they were going to the Princess Theater to be tried for the part of "Alice", in "Alice in Wonderland", and she asked for their hair-ribbons, explaining to Nana that it helped if they looked like Alice. She tied Winifred's brown ribbon first, and then Nana gave her Pauline's black velvet that they had bought in Harrods to match her frock. Miss Jay took a comb and swept Pauline's hair off her face, and tied it back, then she laughed and said she looked ridiculously Tenniel. Pauline was just going to ask her what Tenniel was, when she remembered he was the artist who had done the first "Alice in Wonderland" pictures. Doctor Jakes had told her so.

They drove to the stage door of the theater, and went on to the stage, which was crowded with people. Eight were girls with their hair tied just like Winifred's and Pauline's, so it was obvious they wanted to be "Alice" too, and there were a troupe of children in practice-dress and ballet shoes, and a lot of grown-up people. Miss Jay asked Nana to comb the two children's hair, and she told them to change into their ballet-shoes and to take off their coats; she herself dis-

London County Council.

EDUCATION OFFICER'S DEPARTMENT.

APPLICATION FOR LICENCE

Return to
The Education Officer,
The County Hall,
Westminster Bridge, S.E. 1

THIS FORM SHOULD BE IN THE HANDS OF THE LOCAL EDUCATION AUTHORITY, DULY COMPLETED, NOT LESS THAN FOURTEEN DAYS BEFORE THE LICENCE IS REQUIRED.

Parent, guardian, or person liable to maintain or having the actual custody of the child to whom the application relates, giving relationship to the child.

Name *Sylvia Brown,*

Address *999, Cromwell Rd. London, S.W.*

Relationship *Guardian.*

Employer of the child ... ...

Name *Princess Theatre Ltd.*

Address *Shaftsbury Avenue London.*

We, the above-named applicants, certify that the child, is resident in the area of the above-named Council as local education authority for elementary education, and hereby apply that a licence may be granted to the above-named employer for the said child to take part, *on week-days only,* in an entertainment or series of entertainments known as *Alice in Wonderland* from the period of *five weeks* from the 26th day of *December* 1931,

for a period of *five weeks*

under Section 22 of the Children and Young Persons Act.

We forward, herewith, documents relating to the said child in accordance with the note appended to this application, and we certify that the following particulars are correct:—

(1) Full name of the child ... ...

Pauline Fossil.

(2) Address of the child ... ...

999. Cromwell Road. S.W.

Note.—If this is not the permanent address, the permanent address should also be given.

(3) Date of birth of the child ... ...

December 9th 1920 (approx: see evidence of age attached)

(4) How has the child been educated during the last twelve months? If at school, name the chools.

At home under coaches...

(5) *How* is the child to be educated while employed? If not at a public elementary school, give particulars of the proposed arrangements.

At home under coaches.

(6) Particulars of any previous licence granted by a local education authority for the child to take part in an entertainment or series of entertainments, giving the date of the licence, the place at which, and the authority by whom, it was granted, and the period for which it was held.

—

(7) Has any previous application for such a licence been refused by a local education authority? If so, the grounds, if any, of refusal should be stated.

(8) Nature of the entertainment for which a licence is required.

Children's play.
2½ hours each afternoon.

(9) Approximate time for which the child will be on the stage, and, if the times are not consecutive duration of intervals.

(10) Name, postal address, and description (profession and qualifications) of matron or other person who will be in charge of the child while employed. (If not the parent, state whether the matron has been approved by a local education authority, giving the name of such authority and the date of approval.)

Alice Guthridge.
999. Cromwell Road London S.W.
Nurse.
Has been approved. November 29th

State time the child will leave the theatre. *p.m.*

5.30

Signed (1)

SylviaBrown.

Parent, guardian, or person liable to maintain or having the actual custody of the child.

Date Nov: 20. 1931 Signed (2)

John Freyer
for Frances Robinson Ltd
Employer of the child.

appeared through the iron pass-door which separated
the stalls from the stage.

Pauline tried to see where she was, but there was
such a glare from the footlights that it was impossible
to see more than the front row of the stalls, and that
was empty. Suddenly a voice called out of the black-
ness of the theater, "Is Mr. Marlow there?" A man
stepped out from the crowd on the stage, and came
down to the footlights. He held up his hand to shield
his eyes from the glare, and talked with somebody the
children could not see across the orchestra well. The
conversation was all about whether his voice would, or
would not, do for the Mock Turtle. In the end he said
he thought they had better hear him, and he came to
the back of the stage close to Pauline, fetched a piece
of music, and gave it to a man sitting on the stool in
front of the piano. Pauline supposed he would sing
some grand dull song, and was very surprised when he
sang "The First Friend" out of the "Just So" book.
After he had sung he disappeared through the pass-
door just as Miss Jay had done, and for a long time
nothing happened at all. The children in the practice-
dresses limbered up, and did a few exercises on their
points, which Winifred and Pauline decided they did
very badly, and the grown-up people smoked; then
once more a voice called out from the theater.

This time it said, "Will all the children whose names I call out step forward, please?" Winifred's and Pauline's names were called, and so were all the other girls with their hair done like "Alice's". They looked at each other to see what they ought to do, and then came down-stage and stood in a row in front of the footlights. They seemed to be there an enormous time while people whispered, and then a different voice said, "Little Fair Girl in black, what's your name?" Pauline was just looking to see if anyone else was wearing black as well as herself when Miss Jay replied, "That is Pauline Fossil". There was a lot more whispering, and then the other children were told to sit down. Pauline felt awful standing by herself being stared at by all the people on the stage, and all those she could not see in the stalls. She would have liked to have wriggled, and stood on one leg, but the Academy training had taught her not to stand just how she felt, so she stood as she did before a class, with her toes turned out, her heels together, and her hands clasped behind her back. After what felt like an hour, and was really only a few minutes, Miss Jay came in front of the stalls where Pauline could see her. She leaned across the orchestra well.

"They are going to try you. Will you sing first, or do your speech?"

Every boy and girl at the Academy, when they were nearing their twelfth birthday, got what was called "m'audition" prepared. They meant really, "my audition", but somehow habit had turned it into one word. "M'audition" was a speech from a play, or a recitation, and a song which had a dance worked to the chorus, or to a repeat of the tune. If a child was being seen for an acting part, or simply as a dancer, of course he or she only acted or danced, but every child had a full "m'audition" ready. Pauline had Puck's speech from "A Midsummer Night's Dream", and a song called "Springtime is Fairy Time", which had a waltz tune, and so was easy to dance to. She thought a moment, faced with "m'audition" for the first time, and then said she would do "Puck's" speech, for she thought it would be easier to act than to sing, when her voice was wobbly with fright.

The moment she started she stopped feeling frightened. She had worked at the speech for hours with Doctor Jakes; together they had discussed exactly how Puck felt, and how he looked, until just saying the words made her feel that she had turned into a queer little creature who did not belong to the mortal world. When she had finished, Miss Jay called out that she was to ask her Nurse for her music. Pauline turned very red, for she felt all the other children were thinking how much too old she was to have a nurse; she wanted to explain to them that Nana was not really a nurse, and anyhow Posy was still young enough to need somebody to look after her. But of course she could not, so she fetched her music feeling shamed. Although she had seen the Mock Turtle person give his music to the man at the piano, she did not quite like to do that with hers, so she looked at him first to see if he seemed to be waiting for it. He made things easy; he held out his hand and said cheerfully, "Throw it over". He seemed to know exactly what she was going to do, because he turned to the last page, and played a bit and asked her if it was the right time for her dance. Pauline did some little bits of the steps and said it was, then she went to the middle of the stage and sang.

She was very glad when she got to the end of the second verse, which was all the singing there was, for she had not a very big voice, and it sounded to her, in that large theater, like a mouse squeaking.

She did not mind the dance so much though it was on her points, for there was not much of it, but it felt funny dancing in a velvet frock. The dance finished in a pose on the floor, and when it was over, Pauline got up, feeling rather a fool and wondering what to do next. A set dance like that if done at a charity performance ended in applause, and if done at the Academy ended in criticism; but no dance Pauline had ever seen ended in silence. She looked desperately round to see if any face showed what she ought to be doing, and there was Winifred making tremendous signals at the chair next to her. Thankfully Pauline ran to it, and sat.

"Was I all right?" she whispered.

"The acting was," said Winifred. "You were out of tune in the song, though, and your ankle shook awfully in the arabesque."

Pauline made a face.

"I knew it did. I couldn't hold it; I got my posture wrong. I didn't know I sang out of tune. Was it very bad?"

"No, only to me, because I know the song."

Miss Jay's voice called out for Winifred, and she got up in an awful flutter, almost snatching her music from Nana.

"Hold your thumbs for me," she gasped at Pauline. "I did for you."

All the children at the Academy believed that holding your thumbs brought luck. The Fossils did not really, because everybody at Cromwell Road, except Cook and Clara, thought it silly; but they had to hold them if anybody asked them to, so Pauline gripped hers. But Winifred did not seem to need any help; she recited "You are Old, Father William", and then sang "Come unto these yellow sands," and then did a most difficult dance. Pauline released her thumbs, and looked at Nana, who shook her head. Neither of them said anything, but they both felt sure that Winifred would get "Alice". Winifred herself did not seem a bit sure when she sat down; she said that being able to do things well did not mean you got on best, and that looks and personality were more important. Miss Jay came back through the iron door, and told them they had finished, and she was taking them home. She said nothing as they went up the stairs to the stage door; but when they were in the taxi she said gently to Winifred that she thought she would be engaged as understudy; they were going to try the other children, but she thought it would be all right. Then she smiled at Pauline.

"They are engaging you as 'Alice', Pauline. It's a wonderful chance."

Pauline was so surprised that she could only gasp, but Nana said:

"But Winifred did the better."

Miss Jay nodded.

"Winifred is the best all-round student the Academy has ever had, but Pauline looks right for 'Alice'."

Suddenly Winifred put her head in her hands and burst into tears.

"She looks right for everything, she always will. Oh, I did so want to get 'Alice'! We do need the money so dreadfully."

Everybody tried to comfort her, but they could not, because there was the fact that Pauline was engaged for the part, and she was not. Pauline stopped being pleased, and felt miserable; she thought of Winifred's father, and her five brothers and sisters, and even being able to buy back the necklaces stopped being important.

Before Sylvia could sign a contract for Pauline she had to have a license for her from the London County Council, permitting her to appear on the stage. The first step to acquiring a license for children is to get their birth certificate, which is quite a simple thing to do; but Pauline had no ordinary birth certificate, for, of course, she did not have it on her when Gum found her floating on a lifebuoy, and since nobody knew whose baby she was, they had not been able to get it for her. Fortunately, Gum was a man who believed in things belonging to him being kept in order, and a baby without a birth certificate was not a baby in good order, so he had rectified matters by going to Somerset House, and having her entered as an adopted child. After that she had a birthday, and her birth could be properly certified. It was a mercy he had; for without proof that she was twelve, she could not have been granted a license.

Sylvia obtained from the Education Officer's department of the County Hall a copy of the London County Council's rules for children employed in the entertainment industries. They were all good, and framed to look after the employed child's health and well-being. She filled in the application for a license, and sent it down to the Princess Theater, and somebody for the Princess Theater signed those bits that concerned them. A week later, Sylvia got a letter telling her to bring Pauline to the County Hall on the following Wednesday, with her certificate of birth, to be examined by the medical officer, and interviewed by somebody in the Education Department.

Various people were nervous over this letter. There could be no doubt that Pauline was in the most bounding health, and rather ahead of her age from an educational point of view; but Doctor Jakes and Doctor Smith fussed inside themselves in case she should not be up to the required standard, and miss playing "Alice" through their faults. Nana knew that Pauline ate well, and slept well, and had as well-behaved an inside as any inside could be; but she was haunted

by thoughts of the medical officer of health saying:
"Who has had charge of this child? She has been very
badly looked after." Sylvia could not eat for fear the
representative of the Education Office should look at
her with scorn as one trying to make money out of an
adopted child. On the day of the interview, Nana
cleaned Pauline's reefer coat, and blue beret, and laid
out her newly-washed jumper and some well-mended
gloves, and when she was dressed said with a sigh:

"You may not look smart; but you do look neat."

Mr. Simpson drove Sylvia and Pauline to the
County Hall. He tried very hard to cheer them up,
but they were both silent with fright. They did not
feel any better when they got to Westminster Bridge
and saw the County Hall ahead of them. Really, going
into it looked very like going into Buckingham Palace, it was so large and magnificent. Mr. Simpson did
not care a bit how grand it looked; he swept in at the
front entrance, passed the policeman, and stopped his
car right against the flight of stone steps leading into
the main door.

"Do you think," Sylvia asked in a trembling voice,
"that we ought to have come to this door?"

Mr. Simpson gave a proud look at the door, and
said that in a way it was his, it belonged to the rate-
payers, and he was one of them. This made Pauline

feel a bit better, and she was not as crushed as she might have been by the enormous hall surrounded by commissionaires that they walked into. The commissionaire they spoke to, however, proved to be a friendly man; he looked at Sylvia's letter, and seemed to know at once where she ought to be, and sent them to the lift. The liftman was as nice as the commissionaire, and took a lot of trouble to get them to the right room; but in spite of all this niceness both Sylvia and Pauline wished they need not knock on the door.

All their fuss was for nothing. The medical officer was just like their own doctor, and after examining Pauline, he laughed and said if he looked at her for a year he did not think he would find anything wrong. Pauline was a bit insulted by this, and told him that she had had measles once, and influenza twice. He laughed more than ever at that, and told Sylvia that he wished all mothers could produce as good a specimen as her ward. The Education representative was just as nice. He was very interested, when shown Pauline's certificate of birth, in her story, and so Pauline told him about Posy and Petrova, and he said he should be looking forward to meeting them when their time came for licenses. He asked Pauline questions about her work, and she told him about Doctor Jakes and Doctor Smith. He read the letter they had sent, and then said she was a most highly educated person, which was a good thing for somebody who was going to play "Alice in Wonderland," whom he had always thought a most well-informed child; what other child, he asked, who fell through a rabbit-hole would remember that she was likely to end up in New Zealand or Australia? He asked Sylvia what arrangements were being made for Pauline to go to and from the theater, and she explained that though there would be a matron in the theater, she could not let Pauline be alone, and that Nana was going with her to every performance, unless she went herself. The only part of the interview Pauline did not like was the part concerned with money. As "Alice" she was to earn four pounds a week, just as Winifred had said she would. The rule of the County Council was that at least one-third of a child's earnings must be banked each week in the child's name in the post office, and the post-office book must be shown to prove that that much had been banked, before another license could be granted, which, as a license only lasted three months, was a safe way of seeing it was done.

Pauline, who had read the rules, had worked out that twenty-six shillings and eightpence would go into the post office each week. Eight shillings a week would go to the Academy, who got ten per cent of her earnings for five years because they had trained her for nothing. That left two pounds five shillings and fourpence a week for Sylvia, and for paying back the necklace money. Pauline had decided that Sylvia ought to have thirty shillings a week to help with the house, and that would leave fifteen shillings and fourpence for the necklaces, which would buy back Posy's and Petrova's and pay six shillings and eightpence towards her own, which was very good indeed. But when the County Council gentleman asked Sylvia about Pauline's bank account, Sylvia said that she would always bank two pounds, perhaps more. Pauline gasped.

"Two pounds, Garnie! Why? You only need to put in twenty-six shillings and eightpence."

Sylvia laughed, and so did the London County Council gentleman, who said her arithmetic was admirable.

"But, darling," Sylvia pointed out, "I want you to have a nice lot of money saved by the time you are grown-up."

Pauline did not know what to answer, not being able to explain about the necklaces, so all the time Sylvia and the London County Council man were talking about lessons during rehearsals, and after the Christmas holidays had finished, she was doing sums in her brain. Two pounds a week in the post office, eight shillings for the Academy, and thirty shillings for Garnie would only leave two shillings for the necklaces. It was most worrying; she could not get home quick enough to discuss matters with the other two and Nana.

Nana disapproved of getting into a fuss before you need.

"There's no need to get into such a state, Pauline," she said firmly when she heard the story. "To begin with, you don't know that Miss Brown will take thirty shillings a week, and second there's a way round every corner if you look for it. Now you leave things to me."

That night, after the children were in bed, Nana drew a chair up to the nursery table and took a pencil and paper, and did a sum. It took her over an hour, because she was bad at sums, but in the end it was finished, and she took the result down to Sylvia. She knocked on the drawing-room door. Sylvia was very pleased to see her, and told her to sit down. Nana smoothed her apron.

"Pauline will be earning four pounds a week in this 'Alice in Wonderland'."

Sylvia nodded.

"I'm saving half of it for her, and I thought with the rest, which is one pound twelve shillings, for eight go to the Academy, we would get her some clothes."

Nana shook her head.

"That's all wrong, if you'll excuse me speaking plain, Miss Brown; and it's not fair on Pauline. Those children look forward to being able to help with their keep while the Professor's away." She sniffed to show what she thought of Gum. "Pauline will want a pound to go to the housekeeping."

Sylvia turned red.

"Nana, I couldn't. I'm managing. The money the boarders pay just keeps us and pays Cook and Clara, and you won't take any money. . . ."

"Time enough to pay me when the Professor's back." It was two years since Nana had let Sylvia give her any wages. "But because you can just manage, that's no reason to hurt Pauline's feelings. She wants to help. Now, what's right is"——Nana looked at her sum——"one pound for you for the house. Ten shillings for clothes, and two shillings a week pocket money for the children. One shilling for Pauline, because it's her earnings, and sixpence each for the others. It's over a year now since you were able to give them anything for themselves." Nana got up. "That ten shillings a week can be paid to me, because there's a bit owing on a dress that I got Pauline for her audition, and it's up to me to see it's paid back. Good night, Miss."

Nana went happily to bed, and so did Sylvia, who slept well for the first time for weeks; for there was no doubt Pauline's pound was needed, however hard she pretended it was not.

XI

Pauline Learns a Lesson

*

Pauline was a great success as "Alice". All the papers said so, and published photographs of her. The children who came to see the play wrote her letters and sent her chocolates, and told her she was wonderful, and the grown-ups in the cast were nice to her, and she could not help seeing that they thought she was good. The result was she became very conceited. Petrova and Posy were the first to bear the brunt of it. Pauline thought because she was the leading lady in the theater she was one in the house too, and of course they were not standing for that. It began with her telling them to fetch things for her, and to pick things up she had dropped. Posy, being good-natured, and not very noticing, did what she asked once or twice. Then Petrova said:

"Has something happened to your legs and arms?"

" 'Course not," Pauline answered. "Why?"

Petrova raised her eyebrows.

"I would have thought a person whose arms and legs were all right would have been able to fetch their own pocket handkerchief, and pick up their own wool."

Pauline flushed.

"Why shouldn't Posy? I get used to people doing things for me in the theater."

Posy looked at Petrova, then they both looked at Pauline.

"It's going to be difficult," Petrova said thoughtfully, "when we are all working, isn't it, Posy?"

Posy nodded.

"All of us being like Queens at once."

Pauline got up.

"I think you're both being hateful." She slammed the door.

As the run of the play went on, Pauline got worse. She was very nice on the stage, because everybody was nice to her, but she was very different at home, and in her dressing-room. She had a dressing-room to herself; but it was arranged that Winifred should sit in it, because although there was an approved County Council matron in the theater for the other children, they were all pupils from a different stage school, and Winifred did not know them, so Nana acted as matron for her as well as Pauline. Winifred's mother brought her to the theater and fetched her home again, but Nana was responsible for her in the theater.

As an under-study she was allowed to leave the theater as soon as Pauline had gone on for the last act; but she had a dull job, especially for somebody as clever as she was, who could have played the part beautifully herself. It was difficult for her not to be jealous, with Pauline having all the fun, flowers, chocolates, letters, and praise; but she managed to pretend she did not mind, and spent all her afternoons knitting a jersey, and talking to Nana. Nana understood just how she must feel, and was very nice to her; but Pauline, getting more conceited every day, stopped being sorry for her, and bragged instead about what people had said, and all the presents she got, and even expected Winifred to fetch and carry for her. Nana was shocked that anybody she had brought up could behave so atrociously.

"Fetch what you want yourself, Pauline," she said. "Playing 'Alice' hasn't lost you the use of your limbs."

"Oh, well, if Winifred won't help," Pauline grumbled, "but I should have thought she'd have been glad to have something to do."

"Winifred and I have plenty to do," Nana retorted. "She has her jersey she's knitting, and I have enough to stitch with what you tear, so don't fuss yourself finding work for us."

Pauline messed about with her sticks of grease-paint.

"I shouldn't have thought there was much harm in asking a person to get something out of my coat pocket," she said nastily. "When I let that person sit in my dressing-room."

"If everybody had their rights," Nana answered quietly, "it would be you sitting in Winifred's dressing-room. Now get on with your make-up, and don't let me hear any more of that sort of talk."

Sylvia was very worried at the effect the theater was having on Pauline, but Doctor Jakes comforted her. She said that the more puffed up Pauline became, the greater would be the flatness after the matinées were over, and that then she would learn that most important lesson for an actress—that today's success is easily nobody at all tomorrow.

"Let her learn," she said, "she'll soon find out."

After three weeks of being bumptious to everybody at home, and to Winifred, it became so natural to Pauline that she became bumptious on the stage. The rule of the theater was that a cotton wrap had to be worn over all stage dresses until just before an entrance. Nana always saw that Pauline's wrap was round her when she went on to the side of the stage, and she hung it up for her when she made her entrance. When Pauline came off after the act, or during an act, she

was supposed to wrap it round her. To start with Pauline
was very good at remembering it, but after a bit she
thought it a bore and left it hanging where Nana had
left it, and the call-boy had to bring it to her dressing-
room. This went on for a day or two; then one afternoon Pauline was skipping off after the first act, when
the stage manager caught hold of her.

"What about your wrap, my dear?"

"Oh, bother!" said Pauline. "Tell the call-boy to
bring it." And she ran to her room.

The stage manager took the wrap and followed her;
he knocked on her door. Nana opened it.

"Good afternoon, Miss Gutheridge. Pauline must
remember her wrap. The call-boy has other things to
do than to run after her, and it is a rule of the management's that she wear it."

Nana called Pauline.

"Why did you leave your wrap on the stage?"

"Why shouldn't I?" Pauline said grandly. "Stupid
things, anyway."

The stage manager looked at her in surprise, as up
till then he had thought her a nice child.

"Stupid or not, you're to wear it."

He went back to the stage.

For two or three days Pauline wore her wrap; then

one afternoon she deliberately left it on the stage after the last act. A few minutes later the call-boy knocked on her door.

"Mr. Barnes's compliments, Miss Fossil, and will you go back for your wrap."

"Tell him 'No'," Pauline shouted. "I'm busy."

"Pauline," Nana said, "go at once when the stage manager sends for you."

Winifred was still in the theater, as Sylvia had invited her to high tea with the children after the matinée.

"Let me go." She jumped up.

"Sit down, Winifred." Nana's voice was quiet. "Either Pauline fetches it herself, or it hangs where it is."

"Let it hang, then." Pauline began to take off her make-up.

After a few minutes there was another knock on the door. This time it was Mr. Barnes.

"Did Pauline get my message?" he asked Nana.

Pauline pushed Nana to one side and came out into the passage.

"I did, and I said I wouldn't fetch it, so please stop bothering."

Mr. French, who was the managing director of the Princess Theatres, Ltd., came out of the "Mad Hatter's" dressing-room, which was next door. He stopped in surprise.

"What's all the trouble?"

Mr. Barnes looked worried, as he hated telling tales. But Nana thought a scolding would be the best thing in the world for Pauline. She told him the whole story. Mr. French looked down at Pauline.

"Go and fetch your wrap at once. I don't make rules in my theater for little girls to break."

Pauline was excited and angry, and she completely lost her temper. She behaved as she had never behaved before. She stamped her foot.

"Get it yourselves if you want it fetched."

There was a long pause, and in the silence Pauline began to feel frightened. Mr. French was a terribly important man, and nobody was ever rude to him. His face expressed nothing, but she could feel he was angry. At last he looked at Mr. Barnes.

"Is the under-study in the theater?"

Nana called Winifred, who came out looking very nervous, for she had heard all that had gone on.

"You will play tomorrow," Mr. French said to her. "Pauline will be in the theater as your under-study."

He went down the passage and never gave Pauline another look.

Pauline finished taking off her make-up, and got

dressed, and went home in perfect silence; her mouth was pressed together. Winifred thought it was because she was angry, but Nana knew it was not. She knew that Pauline was terrified to speak in case she should break down and cry. She certainly was not going to let the theater see how much she cared, and of course she would not cry in the tube. As soon as she got into the house she raced up the stairs. She could not go into the bedroom, because the others might come in, so she went into the bathroom and locked the door, and lay down on the floor, just as she was, in a coat, gloves, and beret, and cried dreadfully. At first she cried because she thought she was being badly treated, and kept muttering, "It's a shame; I didn't do anything." "Anyhow, Winifred's sure to be awful; they'll be sorry." But by degrees, as she got more and more tired from crying, other thoughts drifted through her mind. Had she been rude? Had she been showing off? Inside she knew that she had, and she was ashamed, and though she was quite alone she turned red.

Although Nana closed the nursery door, the other children could not help hearing Pauline's sobs from the bathroom. Nana had told Petrova and Posy something of what had happened, and although they knew that Pauline had got so proud that she would cheek anybody, they were terribly on her side now that she was down, and although they knew Winifred could not help being told to play "Alice", they blamed her in a sort of way. Naturally, with all this, tea was not a very cheerful affair, and Winifred wished more than ever that she was not there, and still more that she could go as soon as she had finished eating; but she could not, as she had to wait for her mother to fetch her home. Directly tea was over, Nana sent them all down to Sylvia.

"Remember, now," she said, "Miss Brown hasn't heard what's happened, so none of you show her anything is wrong. You let Pauline tell her herself."

This made things much better. They played "Rummy" with Sylvia, and so that she should not suspect anything, were more cheerful than even they would have been ordinarily.

As soon as the other three had gone downstairs, Nana knocked on the bathroom door, and told Pauline to let her in. Pauline lay where she was for a few minutes, too tired and too miserable and too ashamed to come out; then she turned the key. Nana put her arm round her.

"Come along," she said, "you'll feel better after a bath and something to eat. When you are in your dressing-gown you can go down and tell Miss Brown all about it."

She treated Pauline just as if she were six instead of twelve, helping her off with her clothes, and even washing bits of her, then she put her in the armchair by the fire and gave her a large bowl of bread and milk.

"You eat all that, dear, and stop fretting. Pride has to come before a fall, and that's the law of nature; you've got your fall, and now you've got to be brave and get up again. What's one matinée, anyhow, and if you think right, you'll be glad in a way that poor Winifred gets a chance one afternoon. She's been very good, knitting quietly." Nana gave her a kiss. "I'm fetching the other two up, so when that bread and milk's gone you can have a chance to tell Miss Brown what's happened."

Naturally Sylvia had supposed something was wrong when Pauline had not come down with the others, and when she saw her swollen face, she knew it. Pauline sat on the fire-stool, and told exactly what had happened. It was a very truthful account. Sylvia heard her without a word, then, when she had finished, she thanked her for telling her, and said she was sorry, of course, but very glad for Winifred. This question of Winifred coming first from Nana, and then from Sylvia, made Pauline feel better; if she had to be punished, it was nice that it gave Winifred a chance.

At the matinée the next day she took a bit of sewing to do, and sat quietly in a corner working. She wished Winifred luck before she went on, and when she heard the "Mad Hatter" congratulating her in the passage outside, she managed to smile, and tell her she was glad, though inside she was not really, as of course she hoped nobody was as good an "Alice" as herself. Just as the last act started, Mr. Barnes came to the door and called her. He was nice; he told her Mr. French wanted to see her, and that though Winifred was very good, they'd all missed her, and would be glad to see her back tomorrow.

Mr. French had a large office, where Pauline had never been before. He was sitting writing at a desk. He told Pauline to sit. Instead she came over to the desk and said politely that she was sorry she had been rude and disobedient yesterday, and that she would not be again. He said that was quite all right; she had done very nicely as "Alice", and that doing nicely in a part always went to an actress's head to begin with. It was a good thing to get that sort of thing over at twelve, instead of waiting till she was grown-up. He then said that Winifred had done very nicely as "Alice" too, and that she might take note of it, because it was an object lesson she might remember always. That nobody was irreplaceable. Pauline looked puzzled, as she did not know the word, so he explained that it meant that you could always get somebody else to act any part—that the play was the thing. "Alice" was just as much "Alice", whether Winifred was acting her or Pauline; Lewis Carroll's words were what mattered. Then he told her to run along; but just as she got to the door, he said that he was having a party of children guests round to see the play tomorrow, and she was not to hurry away, as he should bring them to call afterwards.

That night Pauline told Petrova and Posy about Mr. French. Petrova said she thought it was true, and that though she did not think Winifred would be half as good as Pauline was as "Alice", people who had not seen the play before probably thought her perfect. Posy said that she did not think it was a bit true.

"When I dance," she said, "nobody else will do instead of me; they'll come to see me, and if I'm not there, they'll just go home."

Pauline and Petrova snubbed her, of course, for though it was only a very Posyish way of talking, she could not be allowed to say things like that.

Pauline went to sleep feeling terribly glad the day was over and she would be "Alice" again tomorrow, and, down inside, rather surprised to find how right Mr. French was. It really would not matter terribly if she was ill, and Winifred played for the rest of the run. She pushed the thought back, but she knew it was true.

Petrova went to sleep puzzling over what Posy had just said. She did not believe it was conceitedness when Posy said things like that, but it certainly was when Pauline said them. Why?

Posy went to sleep murmuring, "Two chassés, pas de chat, pirouette, two chassés. . . ."

XII

August

*

Except for two broadcast performances of "Alice in Wonderland", Pauline made no more money until June, but the broadcasting brought back the rest of Petrova's necklace, and besides what went to the post office, and to the Academy, it gave Sylvia two pounds for the housekeeping, and got enough stuff in a sale to make them all Spring coats in light tweed with tweed hats to match.

In June she was engaged as a child in the first act of a grown-up play. It was dull work, as she was the youngest of three children, none of whom had much to say, and since she was only in one act she never saw the whole play, and never knew what it was about. The leading lady was a famous film-star, and she seemed to like Pauline, for on the first night she gave her a magnificent doll and a signed photograph. The children hardly ever went to a film, as they had no money to spend, and Sylvia thought very few of them suitable, so Pauline was not interested in the fact that the gift came from a film star. None of the Fossils played with dolls; but this one was so handsome that they put her on the mantelpiece as an ornament, and called her the Queen of Sheba. She stayed on the mantelpiece about three weeks, and then Nana said, Queen or no Queen she collected dust, and sent her to the Great Ormond Street Hospital. The card that came with the doll, Pauline gave to Clara, who said she was as pleased as if it were a bag of gold, for Clara went a lot to the pictures, and the star in Pauline's play was her favorite actress.

Pauline only earned two pounds ten shillings a week in this play, of which Sylvia put one pound in the post office, and five shillings went to the Academy; and in spite of all Pauline's persuasions, she only took fifteen shillings for the house, so that still left ten shillings for clothes. With it, after Pauline's necklace was redeemed, Nana managed to get them all new outfits for the Academy, made them two cotton frocks each with knickers to match, and gave Pauline sixpence a week pocket money and the other two threepence. Pauline was glad the money was useful, but she was not sorry when the play came off, as, after being "Alice", it was poor fun. During the run of the play she attended one dancing class a day, except on the two matinée days; for, as the play was running in term time, she was not allowed by the London County Council to miss any lessons.

Petrova was now in her last year as a non-working pupil; she would be twelve in the August of next year, and so old enough for a license in the Autumn. She now, besides five hours' lessons a day and two walks, had to practice dancing exercises for two half-hours at home with Theo, and had five hours of dancing lessons during the ordinary week, two hours' dancing class on Saturday mornings, and had to come back after tea on Saturday afternoons for an hour's elocution and another hour's dancing. She had been allowed to drop singing classes, as it was obvious she never would be any use at it. The more dancing she learned the more it bored her. With so much training, naturally she became proficient—in fact, she became technically one of the most proficient pupils in her class. She did the exercises neatly, and remembered the routine of a set dance; her points got strong, and she got well up on them; her knees were splendidly straight—in fact, there was nothing wrong with her work, except that it bored her, and she looked as if it did.

Probably nobody but Mr. Simpson ever knew just how bored she was. Nana had long stopped attending classes, and instead sat in the refectory and talked to the housekeeper. Neither Pauline nor Posy worked with her, and if they had, would have been far too intent on their own work to notice Petrova's. Sylvia never asked if they liked their work; they all looked well; and when she saw them, or took them to the Academy, they never discussed dancing with her, as she knew nothing about it. At lessons Doctor Jakes and Doctor Smith never discussed anything but lessons, except over their beavers, when they talked about things they had read in the papers, and about plays.

Petrova had a thin, pale face with high cheekbones, very different from Pauline's pink-and-white oval and Posy's round, dimpled look; she was naturally more serious than the others, and so, being bored for eight hours in each week did not show on her, as it would on them. It was Sundays that saved her. After morning church she went straight to the garage, put on her jeans, and though only emergency work was really done on Sundays, the foreman always had something ready for her. Very dirty and happy, she would work until they had to dash home for lunch. Afterwards, occasionally, they came back until tea-time; then they washed and popped across the road to Lyons, but usually they went on expeditions in the car.

Those expeditions were their secret; Petrova never even told the other two about them. The best of them were to the civil flying-grounds, where they watched

the planes take off and alight, and often went up themselves. Sometimes they saw some motor-car or dirt-
track races; but Petrova liked the flying Sundays best.
Although, of course, she was years too young to fly,
in bed, and at her very few odd moments, she studied
for a ground license; and although she had never
touched a joy-stick, she knew that when she did, an
aeroplane would obey her, just as certainly as Posy
knew that her feet and body would obey her.

Posy lived for nothing but her dancing classes. She
was exceedingly stupid at her lessons; she tried to
work, but she could only say and understand things
with her feet. Doctor Jakes and Doctor Smith seemed
to grasp this, although never, in the years they had
coached, had they taught anyone quite like her before.
In the Autumn term, just before she was nine, Madame saw Sylvia, and it was decided that Posy should
come to the Academy for half of each day, during
which time she should work at languages for the lessons she was missing. She still taught Posy dancing
entirely herself; but she sent her to Madame Moulin
for French, and herself taught her Spanish, and Russian—not that Posy ever learned to speak any of the
languages, but she was taught them all.

Each term that Posy had been at the Academy
she had measured her feet to see if she could wear the

little shoes her mother had given her; but she had tiny feet, and they were always too big; but that Autumn they fitted. She was very proud of them, not because they were really any better than anybody else's ballet-shoes, but because they had been given her by her mother, and she was the only one with a mother, so it seemed rather grand. She would not wear them for any ordinary lesson; but if Madame said, as she did just now and again, "Beautiful, my child! Do it once more because it pleases me," then Posy would at once run to the bench in the corner, and open her shoe bag, and put on her mother's shoes. The result was that she wore them so little that her feet outgrew them while they were still good. For a long time after they pinched her, Posy refused to own to it, because she did not want them thrown, or given, away. Madame came to her rescue, guessing how she would feel. She said she would like the shoes as a souvenir, and she had a little case made for them with a glass front and hung it on the wall.

Posy was a great pet with everybody in the school. Pauline and Petrova told her it was because she was Madame's pupil, for they did not want her to get proud; but they knew it was not really—it was because everybody liked her. She was a sort of secret about the place; they all knew she must be going to dance very well, or she would not be Madame's special pupil, but since "The Blue Bird" no one had ever seen her work. All the rest of the students appeared in various performances for charity, but she never did. Sometimes they would say to her in the refectory, "Dance, Posy". But all she would do was to give one of her funny imitations of this teacher or that pupil. It made them roll about laughing, but they never saw what she could really do.

That Christmas, Mr. French engaged Pauline for "Alice" again. This year she always wore her wrap, and it was as well she did, for Winifred was not the under-study, as she was dancing as a jewel in the pantomime of "Aladdin", and the child who did understudy her, hurt her foot. She managed to come to the theater and get past the doorkeeper, and as she sat all the evening, nobody saw that she could not walk properly; but it would have been very awkward if Pauline had been told to stay off.

When "Alice in Wonderland" finished, Pauline could not get any more work. She worried about this terribly because they were so poor. The last of Gum's money was almost gone, and when it had quite gone, there would be only the boarders to live on, except what Pauline earned and, by the coming Autumn, Petrova. No one ever exactly said so, but none of them really believed Petrova would earn much. Petrova believed it least of all. Pauline went to Miss Jay about work. She told her, as a secret, how important it was she should get some, and Miss Jay promised to see what she could do; but, as it happened, it was a season with no work for a child. Some of the Academy children went away on tour dancing; but if Pauline went on tour it would not help anybody, and the only acting parts which turned up were for boys, and there were plenty of boy students to take those. Nana and Pauline had a good many anxious talks; Pauline had begun to feel the responsibility of being the eldest, and she, and the other children, had a feeling Sylvia must not be bothered, for what with the house, and the boarders, and making accounts meet, she had enough troubles.

It was rather a miserable summer. They had all grown a lot since the year before, and nothing seemed to fit, and there was no money for any more clothes; then Doctor Jakes had jaundice, and she and Doctor Smith went away for her to convalesce. They paid their rent just the same while they were gone, but they did not want any meals, and there was profit on meals. Then, of course, there were lessons. Sylvia had to give those again, and by now they really seemed to know just as much as she did, and they felt they were wasting time, and she knew they felt it. Pauline was terrified lest, if she got an engagement while the doctors were away, the London County Council would not renew her license, because she was sure that they would not call Sylvia "an approved teacher", as it said on the rules she had to be. By the time the term came to an end they were thankful, the children even more for Sylvia than for themselves; they hated to see her worried face staring at the work they had done, while she wondered if it was right or not.

On Petrova's birthday Mr. Simpson took a holiday from the garage, and invited everybody in the house to a picnic. The doctors were still away, and so was Theo, and Clara was having her holiday; but the children, Sylvia, Nana, and Cook, were delighted to accept. His car was not big enough to take them all, so he borrowed a second one from the garage, and they drove to a wood outside Westerham in Kent. Mrs. Simpson had bought all the lunch, so that Cook had a real holiday too. It was a terrific meal from Fortnum and Mason's, and after they had eaten, they all felt too fat to do anything for a bit. They lay on the pine-needles, and looked at the sun coming through the trees, and felt absolutely contented. Even Sylvia forgot to worry, it was so hot, and the pine-needles smelt so good. Presently Posy got up and took off her frock and sandals, and gave a dance for each of them; she danced Cook making a cake, and Sylvia teaching lessons, and Nana ironing, and Mr. Simpson mending a car, and Mrs. Simpson going to church, and Pauline as a leading lady, and Petrova watching an aeroplane while she got dressed. She made them all laugh till the tears ran down their cheeks and they begged her to stop because laughing made them hot. Cook said she had not enjoyed anything so much since she saw Charlie in "The Gold Rush", and Nana that it was a pity she was bent on being a dancer, as she could keep them all if she went on "the halls"; but Mr. Simpson, though he could not stop laughing, said she was a cruel little devil, and far too observant for her years.

After Posy's dances, Pauline signaled to her and to Petrova, to come behind a tree out of earshot of the grown-ups, because they had not done their vowing, and it was Petrova's birthday.

"I've an idea," she said. "Do you think that we could add to our vows? Something to vow and try and earn money to help Garnie?"

After arguing a bit, they decided it would not do any harm, so Pauline raised her right arm, and said in a suitably churchy voice:

"We three Fossils vow to try and put our name into history books, because it's our very own, and nobody can say it's because of our Grandfathers, and we vow to try and earn money for Garnie until Gum comes home, Amen.''

Petrova and Posy both made faces at her, but they raised their right arms and said "We vow". Then Petrova burst out:

"Why did you say Amen? If you say it, we've got to too, like in church, and then it spoils the 'We vow'."

"I don't know why I said it." Pauline looked puzzled. "It sort of came. We do need money so much, it seemed like a prayer almost."

Posy turned a pirouette.

"If it's a prayer, we ought to be kneeling down." Pauline felt a bit embarrassed.

"I'm sorry; I won't say it next time."

"You can. We don't mind, do we, Posy?" Petrova ran off. "Come on, let's play hide-and-seek until tea."

Tea was a gorgeous affair, with a birthday cake with twelve candles. Petrova was very pleased, as she had not had any proper presents, because neither Pauline nor Posy had any money, and Nana none to spare, and Sylvia had sold all her jewelry; and though Sylvia gave her a book, it was only one of her own, and an old book does not make a very good birthday present.

Nothing had come by the post either, which was disappointing, as both the doctors and Theo usually gave them birthday presents. So a pink-and-white

birthday cake with her name on it, and candles, was
a great comfort. Mrs. Simpson told her to cut it, and
showed her a mark which was where she was to make
the cut. When the slice came out something was
shining in it, and there was a golden half-sovereign.
None of the children had ever seen a gold ten shillings
before, and they thought it the best present any of
them had ever had, though, as Pauline said, it would
be a dreadful thing spending it; but Mr. Simpson said,
if she took it to a bank, she would get more than ten
shillings for it, so it was worth the sacrifice of parting
with it. At the end of tea, Cook handed Petrova her
birthday present, which was a box of crackers; they
were the really good kind with daylight fireworks in
them as well as a cap, and pulling them and lighting
the fireworks made a wonderful end to the picnic. The
last firework was a little ball which, when a match was
put to it, unwound until it was a large twisted snake.
It looked so handsome that they made a stand for it
of two bricks, and put it on the top as a monument to
mark where they had spent Petrova's birthday.

When they got home there were two letters for
Petrova and one for Sylvia. In Petrova's were ten shillings from the two doctors and five shillings from
Theo, and in Sylvia's was a letter from Miss Jay. A
management were putting on "A Midsummer Night's

Dream" in September, and Pauline was to go and see them about the part of Pease-blossom, and Petrova was to be seen for the ballet of fairies.

In bed that night, Pauline said:

"Do you think adding the bit about making money to our vow had anything to do with the letter Garnie got?"

"I don't see how it could have," Petrova pointed out. "It came by the afternoon post, and was written before we vowed."

Posy sat up and hugged her knees.

"It might have all the same; you never can tell what's magic."

XIII

The Clothes Problem Again

*

An August audition for two people put a strain on the wardrobe that it certainly could not stand. There was Pauline's black-velvet frock, but the weather was hot, and it would not look right at all. Nana thought clean cotton frocks would do, but the children doubted it; they admitted they did not know what was worn in August, but they did not think cotton could ever be right.

"Very well, then," Nana said. "You must go in your practice-dresses; they're clean, and done up for next term."

Pauline looked at Petrova.

"Practice-dresses never are worn, are they, Petrova?"

"Not unless we are told to put them on and go as a troupe," Petrova agreed, "which we never would do in holiday time."

Nana sounded cross, as she always did when she was worried.

"Well, what will you wear, then? I can't make clothes out of the air."

Petrova put her arms round her neck.

"Nana, darling, could my birthday money make us organdie frocks like we used to have?"

"What, those white dresses with the frills?"

Petrova nodded.

Nana looked thoughtful.

"How much money have you got?"

Petrova fetched her purse and laid out two postal orders—one for five shillings, and the other for ten—and the Simpsons' gold half-sovereign. She reminded Nana that the gold was worth more than ten shillings.

Nana got a pencil and paper and made calculations.

"We could get a nice organdie for two and eleven. Four and a half yards those dresses take—that's nine yards." She passed the paper to Petrova. "You're good at figures: how much is nine yards at two and eleven?"

Petrova worked it out in her head; it came to one pound six and threepence. They all looked at the money. Allowing for the extra on the ten shillings, they had enough. Pauline and Petrova heaved sighs of relief; but Nana shook her head.

"You're going too fast. What about linings? See straight through you in organdie. You can wear the knickers of your practice-dresses, but you must have slips even if it's only jap."

Pauline fidgeted with her wrist watch.

"How much will they cost?"

"Get something good enough for one and six-three," Nana thought, but she'd need two yards for each of them.

"That's six and threepence." Petrova sighed. "And with the organdie money, that's one pound twelve and sixpence; however good the exchange is the day I change my ten shillings, it won't be worth an extra seven and sixpence."

Nana, however, having got so far as to work out how much the dresses would cost, said she would lend the extra money; they could pay her back out of their salaries, though she insisted that before Pauline paid her back a penny, she must return her half of Petrova's birthday money.

The audition was the next day, so there was very little time to make the dresses, even when the money was arranged. Nana went out at once for the stuff, and as soon as she got back, she cut them out, and Mrs. Simpson, Sylvia, and Cook formed a sewing club to help her. Cook made the slips, Mrs. Simpson whipped the frills, which took hours, and Sylvia made up one dress and Nana the other. They were not absolutely finished until just before they were put on; but when Pauline and Petrova were dressed in them, all the workers, though exhausted, said it had been well worth while; they really did do the house credit. Unfortunately Petrova had started a sty that morning, which did not improve her appearance, but nobody mentioned it.

Mr. Simpson drove them, and Nana, to the audition. It was his share of the work, because the money had not run to new hats, and if he had not offered to drive them, somebody would have had to clean and retrim their summer ones; as it was, they went without any.

Pauline was by now quite used to auditions, and she knew this one would be fun, because lots of the Academy students were there, and they told each other what they were doing with their holidays, and looked enviously at Pauline's and Petrova's frocks, which seemed far nicer than anyone else's. Pauline appeared to be the only child from the Academy about the part of Pease-blossom, though there were two each trying for both Moth and Cobweb. They were surprised that no one had been sent for Mustard-seed, but they supposed the part was already fixed.

The stage was crowded with people, mostly grown-ups; Petrova was thankful to get behind the other students and remain hidden. She would not even face the thought that presently she would have to go out in front of everybody and dance; even thinking of it made her inside feel as though she had swallowed an ice too quickly. She felt, too, it would be a waste of time, as nobody would engage a child to be a fairy who had a sty on her eye.

The audition started with lots of people singing; they sang dull songs, mostly in German and Italian, and the children were bored. The singing seemed to go on for hours and hours, and then suddenly a voice called from the stalls "Pauline Fossil". Pauline jumped; her mind had been miles away. She had been planning what, if she got this engagement, she would do with her pocket money, always supposing there was any after she had put half in the post office and paid Sylvia, the Academy commission, Petrova, and Nana. She knew the Fairies' parts could not be worth much, so she was afraid there would not be anything for her, but it was nice planning how to spend it, if there was.

She got up quickly. Nana straightened her skirts, and she ran down to the footlights. She stood there, while a lot of people talked in low voices; then, as nobody told her what they wanted her to do, she put up her hand to cut out the glare from the footlights, so that she could see who was in front. To her surprise, amongst a row of men, she saw Mr. French. He waved.

"Hullo, my dear."

"Shall I say some Shakespeare?" Pauline asked politely.

He shook his head.

"No, run along." He turned to the other men. "You don't want to hear her, do you?"

Everybody seemed to agree that they did not; but Pauline was not leaving things like that; she needed the work, and apart from anything else there was her frock to be paid for. It was, she thought, very mean to bring her down, and then refuse even to hear her. She spoke directly to Mr. French.

"Please ask them to hear me; I know I would be all right as Pease-blossom; honestly I would."

She heard a laugh that she recognized, and shading her eyes again found Madame at the end of the row of men. She was most surprised: Madame never came to auditions. She at once dropped a deep curtsy, and gave the customary greeting. As she got up she heard Madame say "Yes", and Mr. French told her to come through the pass door and speak to them. Pauline had never been through a pass door before; but she was by now too experienced an actress not to know where it would be, and she ran to the prompt side, and there, sure enough, was the big iron door.

One of the men hanging about the stage opened it for her. On the other side there were four carpeted steps down, and on her right the open door leading into the stage box, in front of her the glass-topped swing doors leading through to the stalls. She opened this door, and came down the row of stalls to where Madame and the men were sitting. Madame held out her hand, and Pauline curtsied again, which was difficult between the seats. Then Mr. French introduced her to the other men, and told her that they did not ask her to recite, because they had nearly all seen her as Alice, and knew she would be just right for Pease-blossom.

At that moment the man at the far end of the row stood up and called out, "Will those children who have come about the part of Moth please come forward?"

The two girls from the Academy, and a boy from another school, came to the footlights. Mr. French pulled down the tip-up seat next to him, and told Pauline to sit. A large man with a cigar on the other side of Madame said he thought it was a good idea to have a boy, and Madame said she thought her girls would look better. In the end the boy was told to recite.

He recited "Prospero's epilogue" quite well, but with a very ugly accent.

"Pity about that voice," the man with the cigar said. "Clever boy; might have under-studied Puck."

They all looked round at a man in the row behind, and asked if the boy's voice was always as bad as that, or if it was nervousness. The man said nervousness, he thought, so somebody suggested they might hear a few separate words out of the play. They told the man to get the boy to say "Hail". The man went to the front of the stalls and leaned across the orchestra well.

"Say 'Hail', Peter."

"Hile," said Peter.

"No. Hail. Hay-Hay-Hay-el."

"Hile," the boy repeated.

All the men in the stalls looked at each other and shook their heads. The man with the cigar told the man in charge of Peter it was no good, and asked Madame to get her girls to recite. They both did, one a speech of Titania's and the other a piece of poetry. Pauline thought the girl who said Titania's speech the best, but the one who said the poetry was engaged. They then called for the Cobwebs. Four girls came forward, all with red hair; one, not from the Academy, was much the smallest, and they told her to recite. She was not very good, but her accent was all right, and she was engaged. Then they asked for Mustard-seed. There was a pause, and then the girl engaged for Cobweb curtsied to Madame and said, "She isn't here." It was then Pauline had her big idea. Why shouldn't Petrova be Mustard-seed? She pulled at Mr. French's sleeve.

"My sister is here; she'd make a very good Mustard-seed."

He looked at her in surprise, and said that he did not know that she had a sister, and anyhow they wanted a dark Mustard-seed. Pauline explained that Petrova was dark, and begged him to have a look at her.

Petrova, with her skirt hung over the back of her chair so that it should not crease, was gazing at the roof, and flying an imaginary aeroplane on a new route to China. Suddenly, just as she was crossing Chinese Turkestan, she heard her name called. Nana pulled at her arm.

"Run along, dear; they're calling you."

"What for?" Petrova asked stupidly, for her mind was still in her aeroplane.

"Never mind, what for"—Nana said, shaking out her skirts—"just you run and see."

To Petrova, that walk, from her chair at the back of the stage to the footlights behind which sat those fearful people known collectively as "Managers", was about the worst thing she had ever had to do. Her feet felt large, her hands awkward, and her sty seemed the largest in the world. When she got to the front of the stage, things were made worse, because leaning across the orchestra well was Madame, and in her nervousness, as she curtsied, she toppled over, and all the children on the stage tittered. Crimson in the face, she got up; but Madame did not seem annoyed: she only asked gently what Miss Jay had told her to say as her audition piece. Petrova was so horrified to hear she was to recite that she forgot to be shy.

"I'm not reciting, Madame," she said earnestly. "Only dancing, and singing if they insist. Miss Jay wrote that in her letter to Garnie."

"Is this your sister?" Mr. French asked Pauline.

"Yes." Pauline pulled his arm to get his ear nearer so that she could whisper without anyone else hearing. "Don't look at her sty more than you can help; she's never had one before."

"All right," he agreed, "I won't."

Petrova found that no matter what Miss Jay had said, she had to recite. Her "m'audition" was "The boy's speech from Act III, Scene ii, of Henry the Fifth." Nobody who was taught to speak Shakespeare's words by Doctor Jakes could do them badly, but Petrova had only worked on the speech with her a short time before she went away with jaundice. Even so she had far more idea of the characterization of the boy than she would have had if she had only worked at it during Miss Jay's Saturday class. She stuck her hands into her sash, put her legs apart and started, "Young as I am, I have observed these three swashers". She got along swimmingly until the end of the part that describes "Pistol". She knew the next bit was about Nym, but all she could remember was "For Nym . . ." She looked desperately round for inspiration, and just as she did so Pauline came to her rescue. She knew the speech perfectly. She slipped out of the stalls and into the stage box which was close to Petrova's left ear. She leaned forward.

" 'For Nym'," she prompted, " 'he hath heard that men of few words are the best men'."

The moment Petrova saw Pauline, and heard her prompt, she not only remembered the rest of the speech, but said it far better; it was wonderful what a comfort it was to have her so close that she could touch her.

When she had finished, Pauline went back to her seat and Petrova stood about feeling awkward again; but she had not long to feel awkward, for almost at once Pauline came flying through the pass door, her eyes shining. She dragged Petrova into a corner.

"We've got them. We've got them. We've got them. We're both engaged, me for Pease-blossom, and you for Mustard-seed."

The man with the cigar came to the footlights and called out he was sorry he had to go, and that would be all for today, and would those people he had not seen come at the same time tomorrow?

Pauline and Petrova ran to Nana.

"Imagine, Nana," Pauline said, "both of us and in one play. Could anything be more convenient? Me Pease-blossom, and Petrova Mustard-seed."

They got up to go, and at that moment an awful thing happened. The door on to the stage was pushed open, and in flew Winifred. She was looking less nice than usual, for her hair wanted washing, and she had on a cotton frock which needed ironing.

"Am I too late?" she gasped. "I was at Canvey Island, and Mother only got the letter today—they forgot to forward it. Am I too late?"

"What for?" asked Pauline, with a wormish feeling inside.

"Mustard-seed. Miss Jay wrote that she had especially recommended me".

Pauline looked at Petrova; then without a word they ran to the footlights. But it was no good looking for the managers; they had all gone.

They came back to Winifred.

"I'm sorry," Petrova said. "But I've got it. I didn't know it was you who wasn't there, and now the managers have gone. They gave me Mustard-seed."

Winifred bit her lip. Then she threw back her head.

"It's all right, Petrova; good luck. If it had to be anyone but me, I'm glad it's you." Her voice wobbled at the end.

Nana patted her hand.

"That's very nicely said, Winifred. Now you come back with us to tea, and we'll fix things so that you come round tomorrow, and I'll iron up Pauline's frock for you to wear at the audition, so that you're sure to get into the fairy ballet."

Petrova looked at Pauline, for she knew she was fussy about her clothes, but Pauline was thinking only of Winifred.

"If Mr. French is there, go down and see him. Perhaps he'd get you the under-studies."

Nana caught hold of Pauline as they were leaving the theater.

"I hope you don't mind her wearing your frock, dear; but the poor little thing would never get taken on looking like that. Fairy indeed! She'd be lucky to get into a ballet of goblins looking the way she does today."

XIV

"A Midsummer Night's Dream"

*

THE "MIDSUMMER NIGHT'S DREAM" was a tremendous production; it was far grander than "Alice in Wonderland", or even the play with the film star, and Pauline kept telling Petrova that she must not think the stage was always like that. In "Alice in Wonderland", Pauline's dress had been made in the wardrobe; in the film-star play they had taken her to the children's department of Debenham and Freebody, and bought her a frock ready made; but in this production they were sent to famous stage costume-makers and designers.

As soon as Pauline and Petrova said who they were, large colored pictures were produced, one marked "Pease-blossom", and the other "Mustard-seed". Pauline had hoped their dresses would be the real fairy sort, with wings sticking up behind; but they were not a bit like that. They both had skin tights all over, Pauline's in flesh color, and Petrova's mustard, with queer turn-up-toed shoes to match. Round Pauline's waist and over one shoulder were pink flowers; she had a wreath of the same flowers round her head. Petrova had nothing on beyond her tights, except a funny little hat. They both had silk wings that fastened to their shoulders and wrists, and were so long that when they were walking they trailed on the floor like a train. Nana, who had taken them to the fitting, was disgusted and said so.

"Fairies! Might just as well send them on the stage in their combies!"

The dressmaker laughed.

"Would you have liked frills, and tinsel, and wired wings, and wands?"

Nana turned the picture of Mustard-seed's dress round towards her. Her face showed exactly what she thought of it.

"Combies of a nasty yellow shade is not what a fairy would wear."

"They're modern fairies," the dressmaker explained.

"Modern!" Nana gave the sort of sniff she gave when she thought of Gum. "If that's modern, give me the old-fashioned kind."

Pauline said nothing, but she agreed with Nana. Petrova said nothing because she was not listening. She was wondering if tomorrow, being Sunday, she and Mr. Simpson were going to fly.

The production was on a very large scale—there

was a great deal of every sort of person. There were over a hundred fairies in the ballet——so many that in spite of the fact that Winifred was in it, though she had not got the under-studies, she was quite difficult to find. There were eighty Amazons attending on Hippolyta, and a large crowd attached to Theseus's Palace.

The result of all these extra people was that the principals became unduly important. In "Alice in Wonderland" everybody, except the under-studies, was a principal; the same applied to the film-star play; but in this production there were twenty-one speaking parts, one singing part, and one principal dancer, and everyone else was in the ballet, or walking on. Pauline and Petrova were, of course, principals, and as such separated from the ballet and walkers-on, as if they lived in different worlds. They were so grand compared to the hundred fairies that they might have got proud, if Pauline had not been cured of getting proud, and if Petrova had cared about being a principal; as a matter of fact, except for the money, she would have far preferred the ballet if she had to be in the play at all, as it was less conspicuous. In any case, both of them had too much sense not to know that it did not matter much who played the fairies; they had so little to do that any child in the ballet who had a decent accent could have taken their places in a minute.

As a matter of fact, there was an awkward moment when somebody else very nearly did take Petrova's. It was at their first serious rehearsal—that is to say, nobody had a book—and the producer began insisting on having the inflections and emphasis of a line right. They were called for Act III. The four fairies sat happily watching the clowns at their rehearsal, and Puck putting the ass's head on Bottom, only they had no properties, so there was no ass's head. Then, when Bottom sang, and Titania woke up, they all four stood up ready to make their entrances. The producer stopped the rehearsal and came over to them.

"Look here, I want you three, Cobweb, Moth, and Mustard-seed, to get exactly the same inflection on the 'and I'. 'And I'." He spoke the "and" on quite a low note and the "I" was almost a squeak. He turned to Pauline. "I want your 'ready' on the same high note that the other three are going to use for the 'I'. Do you understand?"

They all said they did, so the rehearsal went on.

The inflection was not difficult, but it was unnatural. Pauline was sent back three times before she got her "Ready" quite right. Cobweb had to say her "And I" four times, Moth, profiting by Cobweb's lesson, got hers near enough to pass for a first attempt; but listening to them all had confused Petrova, and in her effort to do it nicely she made the "and" a growl, like a bear, and the "I" a shrill squeal. Everybody laughed, except the producer, who said coldly:

"Go back and say that properly. This is not the moment to be funny."

Petrova went off stage, but her knees knocked together. Funny! Nobody ever was so anxious not to be funny.

" 'And I'," she bleated. This time there was no inflection at all; both words were on the same note.

The producer tapped his foot.

"Come along, my dear, I have no time to waste, there are plenty of other children in the theater who could play this part." All the fairies in the ballet who were sitting in the stalls sat up hopefully. "Go on, try again." As Petrova passed her Pauline touched her hand comfortingly, but nothing could comfort Petrova.

" 'And I'," she muttered. " 'And I'."

"Make the whole entrance again," said the producer. "That'll help her."

Titania held out her arms.

"Pease-blossom! Cobweb! Moth! and Mustard-seed."

Pauline jumped on to the stage.

"Ready." Her inflection was perfect.

"And I. And I," said Cobweb and Moth.

"And I," said Petrova.

How she did it she had no idea, but somehow her inflection got the wrong way up: her "and" was a squeak, and her "I" a growl. There was an awful pause: nobody dared laugh with the producer already so annoyed. The child who was understudying the four fairies got ready to jump out of her seat and run up on to the stage. Petrova hung her head, while her face got redder and redder; she turned her eyes up to the producer's face. She knew she must be going to lose the part—she wondered she had kept it so long considering her sty was not quite gone—but now this on top of the sty must settle it. Obviously a person who had a part ought to be able to say an easy thing like "and I" right. The producer stared down at Petrova, looking at her sternly; then suddenly his face began to wobble, starting at his chin, then his eyes crinkled up, and then he threw back his head and roared with laughter, and all the theater laughed too. He rumpled Petrova's hair.

"You are a joke." He looked at Pauline. "Sisters, aren't you?"

Pauline nodded.

"Well, take her home and go over it with her till she does get it right. If it's wrong tomorrow I shall have to take the part away." He rumpled Petrova's hair again. "Don't worry, you'll get it."

It was not Pauline who got the inflection right, but Doctor Jakes, who had just returned, recovered from jaundice; and she not only got that line right, but suggested that, as she had nothing to do while the children were at rehearsals, she should take them to the theater. This left Nana free for Posy, and she would enjoy the rehearsals, since it was her beloved Shakespeare, and she could help the children better if she heard what was expected of them. As a matter of fact, after that one rehearsal they had no more trouble.

Almost as soon as rehearsals were under way, official school term began again. This meant there were no rehearsals for the children in the mornings, and that five hours' lessons a day had to be fitted in, as well as a walk, and the afternoon rehearsals. Pauline did not mind; she found the actual being in a theater fun, and though, as a child in the theater, she was strictly looked after by not only one of the two approved matrons, but by Doctor Jakes, she somehow succeeded in enjoying herself. She would sit entranced in the stalls hearing the grown-up people work at their parts. There was no need now for Madame Moulin to quote that an actress can always learn till her last hour. Pauline would be fourteen in December, and not only had the sense to see how much she was able to pick up from watching other people, but she had sufficient technique to follow the producer's reasoning. She understood "tim-ing"; she was still apt to time wrong herself, but she was learning to hear when somebody else timed a line wrong. She was beginning, too, to grasp the meaning of "pace". The producer of "A Midsummer Night's Dream" was a great believer in "pace", especially for Shakespeare. Pauline, listening to the rehearsals, could feel the pace of the production, and going home on the tube she and Doctor Jakes would have discussions about it—how this actor was slow, and that one had good "pace".

Petrova knew nothing of the technicalities of acting, and cared less; she just knew that "timing" was saying a line at the right moment, instead of the wrong, and that "pace" was picking up your cues properly, and she felt thankful that Mustard-seed said so little that once she had the "And I" speech right, she could not go far wrong. She thought the rehearsals a frightful bore, but she brought her handbook on aeroplanes with her, and when not wanted for the fairy scenes, or to work at one of the innumerable ballets, would curl up in a corner, and study it.

One day they got a special call for five o'clock, and there they learned a thing which pleased Pauline, and made Petrova take an entirely different view of re-hearsals. They were to fly—Oberon, Titania, Puck, their four selves, and some extra fairies. The flying apparatus was on small trolleys in charge of men in the gallery from which the scenery was lowered. Petrova, who was ignorant of theater terms, called them "Men up in the roof", but Pauline said correctly that they were "in the flies".

Before flying they were fastened into small harnesses, to the back of which was fixed a wire. Petrova had hoped, when she heard that she was to fly, that she would be held up in the air by a wire, and could propel herself where she liked. It was not nearly as easy as that; but it was tremendous fun. Each actual flight any of them made, was done from a fixed point to a fixed point, which was managed by the angle of the wire to the trolley overhead. They could fly in any direction, because the trolley moved all round the flies; but they could not fly at all except on an arranged cue to an arranged place.

Pauline, Petrova, and the extra fairies, trained as they were as dancers, in no time picked up the way to make a graceful flight; but the grown-ups had great difficulty. Oberon was a brilliant actor but a clumsy mover, and did not look a bit like a fairy king, but more like a sack of potatoes being lifted on a crane. Titania used her arms stiffly and awkwardly. Puck wanted to do strange Puck-like movements in the air, which were good ideas when they were in his head, but looked rather silly on the end of a wire. The whole flying rehearsal was more like a game than work, they laughed so much.

Petrova, with her birth certificate and two photographs, had, of course, been to the County Hall, to be examined for a license. Pauline came too, as the three months allowed on her last license had long ago expired. Sylvia had a joint letter about their work from Doctor Jakes and Doctor Smith. This being Pauline's fourth license, she and the County Council authorities were old friends. They knew this was the last license she would need, and said they hoped she would go on with her savings-bank account. Petrova, though she was quite strong, did not look anything like as well as Pauline, as she was naturally thin and rather sallow. The doctor could find nothing wrong with her, though he took a long time examining her; but he told Sylvia she must be careful of her hours of rest, and horrified Petrova by suggesting extra milk. She had not Pauline's way of expecting everybody to be a friend, and was terrified by the London County Council man, and answered all his friendly questions with monosyllables, which made her sound bad-tempered, though she was not; only embarrassed at so much attention focused on her.

"There," said Pauline, when they got outside. "I told you there was nothing to be frightened of. Aren't they nice?"

Petrova did not answer; she felt glad to have got her interview over, and her license granted. She admitted in her mind that they were as nice as any people could be who had to examine you all over, and stare, and ask questions, but she was not feeling good-tempered enough to admit it.

There was a répétition generale of "A Midsummer Night's Dream"—at least, that was what the papers called it. Pauline and Petrova called it a dress rehearsal to which you could invite friends. The people invited by the management sat in the stalls, the friends of the principals in the dress circle, and the rest of the theater was for those holding tickets from the ballet and walkers-on. Pauline and Petrova were each allowed to invite two friends. Nana would be behind with them, and Mr. and Mrs. Simpson were away, so they asked Sylvia, the two doctors, and Posy. Theo had a seat in any case, because many tickets were sent to the Academy, as so many of the children were supplied from there. To begin with, Nana and Sylvia said that it was too late for Posy, and they could not think of allowing it; but Theo, hearing they were all going, and not the argument about Posy, managed to get seats in the pit for Cook and Clara. That settled it; Posy could not be left in the house alone, so she was allowed to come on the understanding that she went home when the others did, before the last act.

It was a lovely dress rehearsal. If there was any truth in the supposed superstition that a good dress rehearsal means a bad first performance, then the first night of "A Midsummer Night's Dream" ought to have been the worst in history. Never was there a production where so many things could have gone wrong. There were various traps and springboards for Puck, there were gauzes which hid Oberon, there was a most elaborate lighting plot, there were difficult cues for the singers, done by lights because they were out of sight of the conductor's baton, there was the flying—there were, in fact, dozens of things which might have gone wrong, quite apart from the usual drying-up due to nerves, and none of them did. From the first note of Mendelssohn's overture, to Puck's "Give me your hands, if we be friends, And Robin shall restore amends", the production was almost faultless, and quite exquisite. It had a real fairy quality, which not only the audience, but the actors, felt.

Pauline, flying over Bottom's head, with her silk wings streaming behind her, and her toe pointed to alight beside Titania, almost forgot to say "ready" when she came down, because she was thinking to herself how like being a real fairy it was. Petrova, who made her first appearance peeping out from a tree, peered between the leaves at what was going on and thought it all very gay, and stopped wishing she was safely at home. In the dress circle, Doctor Smith and Doctor Jakes enjoyed themselves as true Shakespeareans always enjoy themselves, arguing between each act about the reading of the parts, and the way the lines were said. Fortunately they found plenty to disapprove of, or they would not have enjoyed themselves at all. Posy had never been to see a play before. In order that she should enjoy it, Doctor Jakes had taken great trouble to instruct her in the story; in spite of this, she found the lovers a bore, but was entranced by the rest of the play. She was most impressed by the work of the principal dancer, who, as she explained to Sylvia, was very good. Though forced to dance barefoot—a form of dancing for which she did not care so much as for her work on the point—her elevation was quite remarkable.

"She should be good," Sylvia pointed out. "She has been principal ballerina in revues for quite a while."

"I know," Posy nodded. "Madame told me. That's why I'm surprised she's good."

"You are a snob, Posy," Sylvia laughed. "You've

never seen a revue. How do you know what the standard of dancing is?''

Posy leaned back in her seat.

''It's very low,'' she said seriously. ''When we get
home I'll show you: Madame has shown me.''

''When you get home you'll go to bed.'' Sylvia
looked down at Posy. ''I wish you wouldn't talk in
that rather silly way. You are only ten; you can't know
much about dancing, good or bad.''

''I do,'' said Posy. ''I always shall.''

Sylvia gave up the argument.

''Well, come along; Nana will be waiting for you
in the foyer; the other two must be changed by now.''

In the Pit, Cook and Clara enjoyed themselves enor-
mously.

''It's prettier than that 'Bluebird','' Cook sighed.

They nudged each other every time either Pauline
or Petrova made an entrance. They were not much
impressed by their clothes, though they had been well
prepared for the worst by Nana. Petrova's hat was the
thing that really worried them.

Cook gave Clara an expressive look.

''It's like the hat charabanc parties wear on out-
ings.''

Clara made clicking noises with her tongue against
her teeth.

"It's a shame, that's what it is. Petrova not having the looks that Pauline has, doesn't mean that they've got to make a comic of her."

In the tube going home, Pauline and Petrova pestered Posy for criticism of the production; but the moment she made any, they sat on her, asking her what she thought she knew about it. Nana hurried them to bed when they got in, and told them not to talk. Pauline leaned over to Petrova's bed.

"Do you think you'll like working now you've started, Petrova?"

Petrova thought. She remembered what fun it was flying on a wire, and how much she, Pauline, and the other two fairies laughed in the dressing-room. Then she thought of her handbook on the mechanism of aeroplanes; as long as the play ran she would hardly have time to open it. She turned over in bed.

"Not very much, I don't think."

Posy was considering the routine of the work of the première danseuse.

"You remember where it's getting dark and Derova comes through the trees and dances? I can remember it all but just the end, Pas Couru, Arabesque Developpé, then a Pas de Chat took her off; but there was one move in between. What was it?"

Pauline hummed the music.

"Balancé. Abaisser, then wasn't there a Jeté before the Pas de Chat?"

"You're both wrong." Petrova sat up. "It's not a Pas de Chat that takes her off, it's a Capriole; I noticed most particularly."

Posy stood up on her bed.

"Really, Petrova Fossil. A Capriole! So." She sprang on to her right foot, then jumped and beat her right calf neatly against her left. "Did you see Derova do that beat? And if she didn't, then it wasn't a Capriole."

"She goes off so quickly, you can't see what she does," Petrova argued.

"I can. Pauline's right. Jeté." Posy did it. "Then Pas de Chat. So." She gave another jump, this time with her right leg stretched to second position, then back with the knee bent, she finished almost off the bed with both knees bent, and her left leg across. "Isn't that what she did, Pauline?"

"Almost." Pauline got up. "It's like this, from after the grand Arabesque, Jeté, Glissé, Pas de Chat."

She did it all beautifully, except that the end of her spring took her off the bed and on to the floor with a thump. She scrambled up to get back into bed; but before she was there, Nana opened the door, and turned on the lights. Nana looked at Pauline, and at the state her bed and Posy's were in and she was really annoyed.

"Get into bed, Pauline; and you lie down and behave, Posy. If the London County Council could see you and Petrova now, Pauline, they'd take away your licenses, and I shouldn't blame them. What's the good of them seeing you leave the theater on time, if you play around half the night when you get in? What were you up to?"

Pauline got back into bed.

"Posy asked about the routine of a dance of Derova's and we were showing each other."

"And for why?" Nana tucked Pauline's sheets and blankets into place. "Has either of you been put on to under-study her? If so, it's the first I've heard of it." She moved over to Posy's bed and straightened it. "As for you, Miss Inquisitive, always wanting to know something, you turn over and go to sleep." She patted Petrova's blankets. "You don't seem to have been behaving like a grasshopper, Petrova; but if there's been an argument, I expect you've been in it." She switched off the light. "Now, don't let me hear another sound."

Posy waited until Nana's footsteps had died into the distance, then she raised her head.

"Do you agree it was a Pas de Chat, Petrova?"

"Ssh." Petrova rolled herself up in a ball. "Capriole. I'm going to sleep."

Posy looked at Petrova's shape with dislike.

"Such meanness," she whispered to Pauline.

XV

Independence at Fourteen

*

"A MIDSUMMER NIGHT'S DREAM" was a success. It had been hoped in producing it late in September that it would run until the theater put on a Christmas production. It did better than that: it ran over Christmas with matinées every day. Pauline and Petrova got two pounds a week each as fairies; for the extra matinées they got an eighth of their two pounds, so that they got five shillings extra for each matinée, which brought their salaries up to three pounds a week. They had been putting one pound into the post office, sending four shillings to the Academy, and giving ten shillings to Sylvia for the house, which left six shillings a week for clothes and pocket money. That was not much, with all the clothes they needed. They very seldom got any pocket money, and never more than a penny or twopence. Their extra matinée money came as a surprise; it was in their pay envelopes, and they were not expecting it. A whole pound more! It seemed immense wealth. Naturally two shillings of it went to the Academy; but that would still leave eighteen.

"Do you think, Nana," Pauline asked, "that if we gave Garnie another ten shillings, and you had five for our clothes, we could have the extra for spending; that's six shillings between us, which would be two shillings a week each?"

Nana shook her head.

"I doubt it, dear, with all that's needed for you. What do you want two shillings for?"

Pauline fingered her pay envelope. She hesitated to tell Nana her secret ambition, in case she was told it could not be.

"It's theaters," she explained at last. "I never go to any. I want to see the good people act. I'd like to go to a matinée every week, when I'm not working. I could if I saved up all my two shillings."

"Theaters!" Petrova looked disgusted. "What a waste of good money! If I had two shillings a week, I'd buy books and books and books."

"And what books!" Pauline remarked bitterly, as both she and Posy disliked Petrova's idea of a library. "All dull things about engines."

"Well, there's no need to quarrel about what you'd do with two shillings," Nana put in, "for you won't get it; and if you don't hurry, you won't be out of the theater on time, and that'll get me into trouble with the stage manager, and him with the London County

Council, and you'll find yourselves without a job, and then nobody will get two shillings."

The discussion of the extra pound was brought up at breakfast the next morning. Sylvia, in a way, took Pauline's side; but she insisted that the ten shillings they had planned for the house must go into the post office.

Pauline gave an angry jab at her porridge.

"But that's mean, you know you've got to have the ten shillings, or we couldn't take the two shillings; it's only pretending we could have it if you say that, because you know we wouldn't take it."

Sylvia took a piece of toast.

"There is just one rule that I won't break, and that is that half what you earn goes into the post office."

"It didn't when I earned two pounds ten shillings," Pauline argued. "Only one pound went into the post office, and you had fifteen shillings, and ten shillings bought clothes."

"That's true," Sylvia agreed. "I told Nana that she could have ten shillings for your clothes that once, but I didn't like it; I was quite ashamed of your savings book, when we took it down to the County Hall."

Pauline was red with bad temper.

"Oh, well, if you're going to care what they think."

"I do," Sylvia said quietly. "But I care still more

that you have a nice lot saved for when you are grown up. Now don't let's argue any more about that pound, or we shall all be sorry you are earning it. Ten shillings of it will go into your savings, two shillings to the Academy, five towards your clothes, and two shillings pocket money for each of you."

"Couldn't you have the five shillings instead of our clothes, Garnie?" Petrova suggested.

Sylvia sighed.

"That would be nice; but you want clothes so badly. Nana says that you all need shoes, and Pauline's got to have a coat. Up till Christmas all she's had is two pounds fourteen from each of you, and when you grow so fast, that goes a very little way. She told me yesterday 'A Midsummer Night's Dream' would have to run for months to buy all you need."

Pauline pushed back her porridge bowl.

"I'm not putting any more in the post office." Sylvia, Petrova, and Posy stared at her.

"A child," Posy recited, "has-to-put-at-least-one-third-of-its-earnings-in-the-savings-bank, or-as-much-more-as-may-be-directed-by-its-parents-or-guardian. This-is-the-law. I learned that in French with Madame Moulin. I forget what the French was, but that was what it meant in English."

Pauline looked braver than she felt.

"It's quite right. That is the law; but I'm not a child. I've just had my fourteenth birthday. The law lets me work; I don't need a license, and I can do what I like with my own money."

"Pauline!" Petrova was shocked. "You wouldn't be so mean as to take it all."

"You are a fool." Pauline looked scornful. "You know I wouldn't. But I was thinking in bed last night; here we are, never any money, Garnie always worried, and we never have any clothes. If the money that I always have to put in the post office is spent on the house and us, we'll have enough. All I want is the three shillings a week for ourselves. I know it sounds a lot, but theaters are expensive—even the gallery."

Petrova looked at Sylvia.

"It is a good idea, Garnie. She needn't put any more in the post office, need she?"

"I think it's a very good plan," Posy agreed. "If I have two shillings I shall save it till next summer and go and see the ballet at Covent Garden. I could go often for that."

Sylvia looked at them all in a worried way.

"Do get it into your heads that nobody wants to stop you having two shillings to spend. I have always thought it a shame that Pauline had so little for herself when she worked so hard, and now the same applies to you, Petrova. But it must not come out of the half you save. You give me plenty for the house, I can manage."

"I shall put nothing more into the post office—at least, not until Gum comes home," Pauline said firmly. "And what's more, if we need it, I'll take out what I've saved."

Petrova and Posy looked at her with a mixture of admiration and shocked amazement. If there was anything that was sacred in the family, it was the savings books. The walk to the post office on Saturday mornings was more sure to happen than church on Sunday. Sometimes Nana, after an anxious evening patching and darning, would sigh as she saw the notes swallowed over the post-office counter; but when Petrova one day described the post office as "that nasty office eating my money" she had been furious.

"Right's right, dear, and it's no good questioning it, and don't let me hear you at it again."

Now here was Pauline saying she would put nothing more into her book. That she was fourteen and could do as she liked.

Sylvia got up.

"I shall talk to Nana; she's certain to make you see sense, Pauline. The London County Council don't mean that because they give up watching you that they expect me to as well. I've got to take more trouble, if possible."

Sylvia sent for Nana to come down and talk to her, and the two doctors as well, as they had educated Pauline, and Theo because she taught her dancing. She would have liked to have asked Mrs. Simpson's advice too, but she could not think of any excuse. As soon as they all arrived she told them about the money argument and asked what they thought. To her great surprise they agreed with Pauline; but all for different reasons. Theo, who was just dashing off to the Academy, gave her views first. She said that she thought it was important that Petrova should save all she could, as she saw no future for her in the theater; but that Pauline showed signs that her gifts as an actress were not those of a precocious child; her work was improving, as incidentally were her looks. Theo thought with any luck Pauline should be so successful as not to need her savings.

Doctor Jakes and Doctor Smith did not believe in too much saving. They both believed that with more money in the house there would be a chance for the girls to develop their tastes; it would certainly be good for Pauline to be able to go to the theater now and then. Nana said that she had been feeling in her bones lately there was a change coming. Pauline was getting very independent, and that if it took the form of wanting to help more, she thought she should be given a chance.

Sylvia thanked them, and when they had gone she called Pauline, and told her that she was to have her way.

"Though you know, darling, I'm going to feel dreadful living on you like that."

Pauline took far more pleasure in her salary now that most of it did not vanish into the post office. It was with dismay that two or three weeks later she heard that the notice was to go up the following Friday. Sure enough when they arrived for the performance on the next Friday there was the notice on the green baize board in the passage. Petrova made a face at it, for although the extra matinées had stopped after three weeks, and they now only had them on Tuesdays and Thursdays, Pauline was still giving them a shilling, but if the play came off shillings were bound to end. Pauline did not seem much depressed about the notice when it was actually up, but rather excited instead. When they went down for their first entrance, Petrova wanted to know if anything nice had happened. She whispered because they were on the side of the stage.

"Not yet," Pauline whispered back. "I'll tell you on the way home."

The matron frowned at them.

"Don't talk in the wings, Pauline and Petrova."

In the tube that night Pauline dragged at Petrova by the hand and pulled her into one of the seats for two. The one opposite was full, so Nana had to sit some way off, and could not hear what they said. Pauline spoke quickly, as she was excited.

"That man that plays Oberon."

Petrova nodded. "Donald Houghton?"

"Yes, him. Well, he's putting on 'Richard the Third' as soon as this comes off." She looked at Petrova as if expecting signs of intelligence, but Petrova gave none. "Don't you know your 'Richard the Third'?"

Petrova sighed at Pauline's short memory.

"You know I don't; you only did it because it was in the test examination you did for your school certificate. What about him doing it?"

"The Princes in the Tower are in it."

"Us?"

Pauline nodded.

"I don't see why not. I thought we'd ask him."

"How could we?" Petrova protested. "We only

see him on the stage, and we aren't allowed to go into the grown-ups' dressing-rooms."

"I thought we'd write."

Petrova looked in admiration at Pauline.

"That's an idea. When shall we write it?"

Pauline considered their crowded days.

"Well, we might get Theo to let us off dancing practice if we said it was for something very important; but then Posy would want to know what we were doing; and we mustn't tell anybody or we shan't be allowed to send the letter. We shan't have time at lessons, of course, and then there's our walk, then it's half-past one. Sometimes there's a quarter of an hour after lunch before our other walk; if there is, we could do it then. If there isn't we'll have to ask the doctors to give us ten minutes out of after-walk lessons, for there's never a minute between them and tea-supper before we go to the theater."

"How about us both writing one in our baths and comparing them? That would save time," Petrova suggested.

The letter which they finally took to the theater next day was the result of snatched minutes. Theo would not let them off practice, but she gave them five minutes at the end before they began lessons.

They got another five minutes after lunch before their walk. Pauline copied the letter out beautifully at evening lessons when she was supposed to be writing an essay. She showed it to Petrova on the tube, and they agreed it could not well be improved upon.

"DEAR MR. HOUGHTON,

"We hear you are going to act King Richard the Third. Would you have us as the Princes? You will not know our names, but we are Pease-blossom and Mustard-seed. We are not supposed to write letters to people in the theater so would you be sure to send the answer before the last act as we go then. Nana who comes to the theater with us won't mind but the real Matrons would.

"Yours sincerely,
"PAULINE FOSSIL."
"PETROVA FOSSIL."

The letter was addressed clearly to Donald Houghton, Esq. At the theater Pauline went ahead with Nana, and Petrova lagged behind. The moment they were out of sight, Petrova rushed the letter across to the doorkeeper, asking him to be sure and deliver it, but not to say anything about who had given it to him. He bowed very grandly and said, "Leave it to me, Miss Fossil." At that moment Nana called Petrova, and she had to race up the stairs.

Pauline and Petrova found the evening almost unbearably long. Each time they came back to the dressing-room they looked round for a letter, and there was not one. They came off after their last entrance and almost cried to find there was still nothing. Gloomily they peeled off their tights, and put on their dressing-gowns, and began to remove their make-up. Then suddenly there was a knock on the door. Nana opened it. Both Pauline and Petrova stopped cleaning their faces and listened.

"Yes," they heard Nana say. "What is it?"

"Do Pauline and Petrova Fossil dress here?" a man's voice asked.

"They do." Nana sounded very uncompromising; they knew she thought they had done something wrong, and was going to deny it if she could.

"Well," the man went on, "Mr. Houghton says, would you bring the young ladies to his room for a minute?"

Cobweb and Moth stopped cleaning their faces. They stared at Pauline and Petrova.

"Well, I never," said Cobweb.

"What's Oberon want with you?" Moth asked.

"Button up your dressing-gowns, dears," Nana interrupted, "and come along. We'll be able to tell these two what he wants when we've found out."

Oberon was sitting at his dressing-table. He turned round as the dresser showed them in. He held out their letter.

"You sent this?"

Pauline nodded.

He smiled at her.

"What makes you think you could play the Prince of Wales?"

Pauline felt very shy.

"We've been taught to speak Shakespeare."

"Who by?"

"A Doctor Jakes. You wouldn't know her."

"She teaches us English," Petrova added.

"All right, then. If she teaches you to speak blank verse, let's hear you." He nodded at Pauline. "You begin."

In a dressing-gown with your make-up not properly off is not a good moment to recite a speech of "Puck's", but, as usual, Pauline had only to begin and she was "Puck". Petrova found the dressing-gown and rather smeared face a great help for the boy in "Henry the Fifth". When they had finished, Oberon shook them both, and Nana, by the hand.

"The casting doesn't rest entirely with me," he

said, "but I'll do what I can; I can't promise more. Good night."

Back in the dressing-room Moth and Cobweb were waiting.

"Well," they asked as the door opened, "what did he want?"

Pauline and Petrova said nothing, as they were afraid to say they had been for parts, and they knew if they did every child in the theater would be after them tomorrow. Nana came to the rescue.

"They've been talking in the wings as usual," she said severely. "And it wasn't a lie either," she added as the door closed on Moth and Cobweb, "for I'm yet to hear of the night when you don't talk in the wings. Come on, Petrova, I must get you out of the theater, or I'll have the stage manager after me; and you don't want to have to tell him you're fourteen, Pauline, or you'll be kept till the end of the show, and that'll mean a nice job for someone fetching you home. And when we get on the tube I'd like to hear what all this Prince of Wales business is about."

XVI

"Richard the Third"

PETROVA could not get to sleep. It was all very well
to write a letter asking Oberon to see Pauline and herself about the parts; that had been fun, but now she
was faced with the possibility that they might be engaged for them. She had asked Pauline how much the
"Duke of York" had to say, but Pauline only said
"not much", which might mean anything. She sat up
in bed and looked at Pauline. She seemed very much
asleep, but perhaps she would wake up easily. She gave
her eiderdown a twitch, but Pauline never moved.
Then she gave all the bedclothes a pull, but she lay
like a log.

Petrova lay down again. It was sickening; Pauline
was asleep. If only she knew just how long the part
was she would feel better—it might only be a line,
and if so, she had no reason to worry. She heard the
door of what they called their "sitting-room", and
Nana still would call the "day nursery", shut; that
meant Nana was going to bed. She sat up again. Nana
did not take long going to bed, and once she was there,

only a very little while before going to sleep. There
was the Shakespeare on the shelf; she would find out
about that part for herself.

Half an hour later she put on her dressing-gown
and slippers, and crept to Nana's door. There were
very nosy sounds coming through it; there could be
no doubt she was asleep. In the sitting-room stove
some red-hot ashes still glowed, and in the fireplace
were the coals that Nana had taken from the stove
to save money. Petrova looked longingly at the coals
because it was very cold, but she knew picking them
up in tongs was difficult, and she was sure she would
drop one and wake everybody. Instead she got the
Shakespeare, and lay down on the rug as close to the
guard as she could squeeze.

Lessons with Doctor Jakes had made her quick at
finding her way amongst Shakespeare's plays. She
studied the cast list of "King Richard the Third".
There were the Princes. "Edward Prince of Wales;
afterwards King Edward the Fifth," "Richard, Duke
of York", they were bracketed together. She skimmed
through the pages to see who entered, and came to
the "Duke of York" in Act II, Scene iv. She read the
scene through, then sat up.

"Petrova Fossil," she said to herself sternly, "what

have you done? You've asked for a part you couldn't possibly act."

She took up the book again and re-read the speech that begins "Grandam, one night, as we did sit at supper". She could imagine the producer's voice, "Make it amusing, my dear, you're a small boy. Imitate your Uncle Gloucester's voice." She shuddered to think just how badly she would do it. She turned over the page, and found "York's" entrance in Act IV, Scene i. It was the scene with his brother, the young King Edward. She could see in reading it how good Pauline would be as the elder boy; she would be dignified and say her lines well; but at the same time she thought that young "King Edward" would be a lot easier to act. He did not have that awful habit of playing with words, and scoring off everybody that seemed to come over young "York" every time he opened his mouth. She read on, and came at last to Act IV, Scene iii, where Tyrrell describes the death of the Princes; then she shut the book.

"Well, at least, if the worst comes to the worst and I play the part, they both die soon."

She put the book back into the shelf, and turned out the light; as she did so the clock in the hall struck twelve. As she crept across the landing back to bed, she was struck by the fact that there was a light on downstairs. She leaned over the banisters; it was not the hall light, but came from the drawing-room, where the door was open. "Somebody's left the light on," she thought, and knowing that electric light accounts were some of Sylvia's worst worries, she slipped down the stairs to turn it off. But when she got to the drawing-room, she found the light was meant to be on, for Sylvia was at her desk working. Petrova, sure that she was alone, had not been particularly careful about noise once she was past the bedroom doors, so Sylvia heard her.

"Who's that?" she called out in a quick, frightened voice, for she was expecting no one to be about at that time of night.

Petrova came in.

"Goodness, darling!" said Sylvia. "How you scared me! What are you doing out of bed?"

Petrova sat down in the armchair. There was a tiny fire still alight, and she was very cold; she held out her hands while she tried to think of an excuse, for they had decided not to tell Sylvia about the parts until they had got them, so that she would not be disappointed if they did not. And she certainly could not tell her she did not want to be engaged for it; that would be too mean, with the money so badly needed. She got out of the difficulty by muttering she had been somewhere, and on the way back had seen the light.

"And that's true," she comforted her conscience: "the sitting-room is somewhere."

Sylvia came over to her and felt her hands and feet; she told her she was perished and poked the fire.

"I tell you what we'll do," she suggested—"we'll have a picnic. We'll have cocoa and biscuits. Mrs. Simpson has given me a tin of cocoa and milk mixed, and one of biscuits; I'll go and get them."

She went out, and while she was gone, Petrova began to feel less scared. She now saw it was ridiculous to worry. She need not play the "Duke of York"; she could perhaps send Oberon a letter tomorrow to explain she had made a mistake, and did not want him, and try to get into a dancing troupe instead.

Sylvia came back with the kettle and things on a tray. She knelt by the fire and put the hottest coals together, and the kettle on them.

"I've become quite clever at this," she said, "I've learned the art of boiling a kettle on the tail end of a fire; it's the last thing I do before I go to bed each night."

"Why do you sit up so late?" Petrova asked, while she watched the cocoa and milk doled into the cups.

Sylvia made a face.

"Accounts. Horrible things."

"But you can't have to do them every night," Petrova persisted.

"No."

Sylvia opened the biscuit tin and passed it; they were a lovely mixture, Petrova saw, with all the ones she liked, including gingers and petit beurres. She took two, and looked up inquiringly, for it was obvious Sylvia's "No" was not the end of what she was going to say.

Sylvia found a finger biscuit for herself and broke it while she thought.

"I'll trust you with a secret, Petrova, that I haven't told anyone except Nana. I'm trying to sell the house."

"Sell it!" Petrova gasped. She had always lived in the Cromwell Road and could not imagine living anywhere else. "Sell it, Garnie? Then where'd we go?"

"I don't know, I haven't sold it yet. A flat perhaps."

"What, all of us—Mr. and Mrs. Simpson and everybody?"

"Scarcely. It would have to be an enormous flat for that. No, just ourselves and Nana."

Petrova looked at her indignantly.

"Where are the doctors going, then? Or Theo, or the Simpsons? And what about Cook and Clara?"

The kettle began to boil and Sylvia mixed the cocoa.

"I don't want to sell it, Petrova, so don't be angry with me; but I went to see Gum's lawyers a month ago; all the money he left me is gone. They are trying to trace him, as they think they know where he and his party are, but they are difficult to get in touch with. Meanwhile I have nothing at all except what you children pay me and what I make out of the boarders. But Mr. Legge—that's the lawyer—told me a thing I'd never known before: that this house was bought in my name. Gum bought it soon after I was born, and I suppose he planned to settle it on me."

"And you want to sell it?"

Sylvia shook her head.

"Not want to, got to; they may buy it for part of an hotel, and the money I get will give us something to live on until Mr. Legge can trace Gum."

Petrova sipped her cocoa, and thought how miserable it would be when Mr. Simpson did not live in the house; but she could not be so mean as to say so when Sylvia was hating things so much already; instead she said:

"So that's what you are doing when you sit up at night."

"I'm making an awful thing called an inventory," Sylvia explained. "The house is mine, but what's in it is Gum's, and I've got to put down every single thing in every room." She got up. "Swallow that down; you must go back to bed—I should take another biscuit with you." She passed Petrova the box, and then laid her hand on her shoulder. "Are you liking the work in the theater, Petrova? I know Pauline loves it, and you couldn't stop Posy from dancing; but sometimes I've thought you would rather do something else. We may be poor, but I hope you know that we're not so poor that I would let you do work you weren't happy in."

"What other work could a person of twelve do?" Petrova asked as casually as she could.

"None; but you could give it up and train for something else when you are older."

Petrova's heart, which had bounded, sank again. For one glorious moment she had thought there was a career for girls of twelve that she had not heard of; anything would do as long as it did not mean speaking on a stage. But there was none, and the money she earned was needed. She got up.

"Silly Garnie." She took a bit of biscuit. "You know I love it. Why should I want to do something else?"

Back in bed she considered this statement. That was a lie really, she thought; but in a way it was true.

"I don't want not to act when we need the money. I'd only like not to act if we didn't need it."

She thought of the house being sold, and all the boarders, especially Mr. Simpson, going away; and turned her face on to the pillow, and cried till she went to sleep.

Oberon, true to his promise, had Pauline and Petrova sent for about the two Princes but Petrova need not have worried. The same producer was producing "Richard the Third" as had produced "A Midsummer Night's Dream". He did not hold an audition on the stage, but saw everyone in his office. He told Pauline she was engaged the moment she came in; he explained they had wanted to get boys, but they could not, and she was their first choice if they had to have a girl. The only question was her height. She was small for her age and he had doubted if she would look twelve, but she seemed to have shot up a bit lately. Pauline rather haughtily told him she could hardly help looking twelve, since she was fourteen, at which he laughed, and told her not to be so fierce; she was engaged. But when Petrova was shown in, he shook his head.

"No, my little friend, not again." He laughed. "It would be much worse than 'And I'."

Petrova laughed too.

"I knew it would, but I had to ask to play him."

He looked up.

"Why?"

"Well, you see"—in the interest of conversation she forgot all about her heels being together and her hands folded behind her; she lolled against his desk—"it's the money; our guardian's Great Uncle has gone away and not come back, and until he does we are very poor, so I have to try and get parts."

He lit a cigarette.

"If that's all, I can use you, and you need never say a word; you shall be a page. There won't be much money in it, but . . ."

"I know, you needn't say," Petrova interrupted. "I'm not worth much." They both laughed. "Thank you very much for the page; I shall like that."

"I might give you the under-study of 'York' . . ." He broke off, for her face was so horrified. "Don't you want it?"

"I must have it," Petrova groaned, "if it earns me more, but I'd much rather not. Think how awful to come to the theater every night wondering if you'd have to go on."

"You are a scream," he said. "All right, I was only teasing; I'm not offering you an under-study."

Pauline was really happy as the young "King Edward". Doctor Jakes, who was fonder of "Richard the

Third" than any other of Shakespeare's plays, had great discussions with her about her part.

"You can't look of royal blood, Pauline," she said, "by simply coming on with your head up. Dignity is trained into royal children before they can toddle; graciousness, consideration for others, on unshakable belief in the greatness of their position. You have got to think of yourself day and night like that until you have the reading of your part fixed. You are not Pauline Fossil; you are a boy who has known that one day he must rule, though had not expected to so soon, but who has accepted his position, and is kingly in every movement."

The rehearsals slipped by Pauline like a dream; for the first time she was not acting—she was feeling a part. The child who was playing little "York" was a great talker, and liked to gossip with Pauline at rehearsals. Pauline knew it would sound silly to say "Don't talk to me before I go on, I want to feel like a king"; but she managed to hide before her entrances, and she would shut her eyes, and imagine that the theater was gone, and instead was a street in the old London of 1483. Down it she walked, a King, but a King who was on his guard, who knew himself a defenseless boy. She bowed to the imaginary curt-sying crowd, she drew herself up with dignity hid-

den by courtesy to meet the Lord Mayor and his
train, remembering always that the greedy eyes of
Uncle Gloucester were upon her, and he must not see
she was afraid. In this spirit she managed to be so right
at even the earlier rehearsals, that it did not seem queer
to the nobles and the people to bow and curtsy to her.
So strong was her own belief that she was a King that
they all felt it. Her dress was a black tunic and silk
tights, and she had decorations round her neck and the
ribbon of the Garter round her knee. At the dress
rehearsal, after "York" had gone on to the stage, she
stood a minute staring at herself in a long glass, and
she did not see herself, but "Edward the Fifth", and
as "Edward" himself, not Pauline acting "Edward",
she swept on to the stage.

Pauline attracted a great deal of attention from the
critics as "Edward". Doctor Jakes cut all the notices
out of the papers, and read her those parts that were
about her acting, but not those about her looks. To
save trouble, Petrova was put to dress with the two
Princes, which meant Nana was in the room all the
evening, although Pauline, being fourteen, had no
need of a matron, and Nana had strict orders from
both Sylvia and Doctor Jakes not to allow her to be
shown cuttings. They were afraid that if she read all
that was said about her prettiness, she could not help

getting self-conscious, which at the moment she was not. But certain results came from all this notice which she could hardly fail to see. She was asked for sittings at about half a dozen of the best photographers', which the management insisted on her accepting, as the advertisement was good for the play, and after a bit they began to appear in the papers. Pauline, however, showed no signs of suffering from swollen head. The only thing she was proud about was that she was able to give Sylvia three pounds nine shillings a week, for she earned four pounds, and after allowing one shilling pocket money for each of them, and paying the Academy commission, that was what she had left.

Petrova was quite happy as a page; she had no responsibilities, and she was able to help a little towards the house. She earned thirty shillings a week, of which one pound went into the post office and three shillings to the Academy, and she gave seven to Sylvia. Sylvia wanted to take only four, and the other three to go for pocket money, bringing that up to two shillings a week again. But Petrova was shocked at the suggestion, pointing out that pocket money could only be thought of on a high salary, or if, as at Christmas, there were extra matinées.

"Richard the Third" ran into July, but just before the end of its run the most exciting thing happened.

Pauline was sent for to have a film test. The studio was some way outside London, so Mr. Simpson offered to drive Pauline and Sylvia down, and wait to bring them home. The studios seemed to be almost a town, there were so many vast buildings collected together. They showed the appointment letter to the uniformed man at the door, who seemed to know exactly what to do with them, and gave them to a messenger who ushered them into a large dressing-room exactly like a dressing-room in a theater.

"The make-up room is round the corner to the left, the third door," he told them, and disappeared.

Pauline and Sylvia looked at each other. Pauline had on her black velvet audition dress, though it was rather hot for June, but her white organdie would get so crushed in the car.

"I can't take anything off," she said. "So why do you think they put me in here?"

Sylvia had no idea, but said she thought they had better go to the make-up room and see. They followed the directions and tapped timidly on the make-up man's door. He called out cheerfully "Come in". He seemed to be expecting Pauline, because he wrapped her up in towels without a word, and rubbed some cream into her face before asking who she was.

"You're the little girl, aren't you?" he said at

last, "playing in the Shakespeare along with Mr. Houghton?"

"That's right," Pauline agreed. "But I can make myself up, you know."

"In the theater, yes," agreed the man. "For the pictures, no. You use grease-paints, don't you?"

"A little," Pauline said. "Number five with a little eight for background and . . ."

But the man was not interested in what Pauline used for her face on the stage; instead he held up a tube.

"But I use Max Factor, and that's different."

It was different, Pauline found. Instead of a stick of grease-paint, it was a paste which was massaged into the skin and allowed to dry on. When he had finished with her, her face looked most unlike itself, and she did not think much of it; but she thanked him politely, and asked where she should go next. He told her to go back to her room, and she would be sent for.

A messenger came to fetch her. He said she was to go to studio three, where they were waiting for her on the floor. Pauline was a bit puzzled at this, as she could not imagine where people should stand except on the floor; she had yet to learn that in film jargon a floor was a stage. Pauline was too used to auditions to be very nervous, and never having faced a movie camera before, she was not as scared by it as she would have been if she had known more about it. A man, whom everybody called Mr. Sholsky, shook her hand and told her what he wanted her to do. They were not difficult things, and all different. Once she came into a room, and sat on the arm of a chair in which Mr. Sholsky sat, and answered the questions he asked her, and another time she had to look for something hidden amongst the papers, and read one of them. Nothing difficult, but all rather confusing because of the bright, hot lights, and the crowds of men on the cameras. There seemed to her to be a fearful lot of time wasted. Before each little thing that she was told to do the same routine was gone through. Suddenly all the lamps would be switched on, and the cameras start to whirr, then a boy came in front of the set, facing the cameras with a board on which was written in chalk: "Pauline Fossil. (Test.) Director, Mr. Sholsky. Camera, Mr. Lewis. Sound, Mr. Part. Take". In front of the word "Take" were two wooden slots into which were slipped number One, Two, Three, Four, etc. After standing in front of the camera for a moment the boy clacked two wooden clappers together, and ran off. There was a moment's pause and then Mr. Sholsky said "Action", which meant Pauline had to start. Each time she had finished what she had been given to do, the lamps were switched off, and the cameras stopped turning, and the camera-man and Mr. Sholsky had a whispered discussion, after which someone rang a telephone bell and asked "O.K. for sound, Bill?" After some minutes the answer came back "O.K. for sound", and Mr. Sholsky told Pauline what to do for the next take.

When at last they had finished with her, Mr. Sholsky walked back to the dressing-room with them and told them they were looking for a girl to play Charles the Second's sister in a big film about Charles the Second. They were not using the grown-up Henrietta much, but her childhood as an exile in France. He told them he was testing a great many girls for the part, but that it would do no harm for her to read up Charles the Second's reign, just in case she was engaged.

Mr. Simpson drove them home very quickly, but not quick enough for Pauline, who was longing to get at Doctor Jakes and say, "Tell me all about Charles the Second's sister Henrietta."

XVII

Making a Picture

*

AUGUST always seemed to be an unlucky month in the family, and this one found them in a worse state than usual. No one had any work, and there was none in prospect, unless Pauline was engaged to play Henrietta in the film, and that seemed a remote chance, as it was seven weeks since her test and they had heard nothing. Pauline was very worried, and would stare anxiously at herself in the glass.

"It's an awful thing, Nana," she said, "if my face is no good for the films, for it's difficult to be in permanent work in the theater, and films do pay so well."

Nana sighed.

"It's very worrying," she agreed. "We were all saying when you went for your test that you ought to do well. Clara says you are cut out for it, and she ought to know, seeing the time she spends at the Pictures."

This year there was no picnic for Petrova's birthday. Mr. and Mrs. Simpson had gone to Eastbourne, and the two doctors to the cottage on the Common in Kent, where they had all been to convalesce after whooping-cough, and Theo to a dancers' congress in Germany. Cook was away for her holiday and Clara running the house, which meant that everybody had to help a good deal. The girls loathed helping in the house, and Pauline and Petrova felt it an injustice they should be asked to in their holidays, when they had been earning the family income for months past. They grumbled and argued until Sylvia, Clara, and Nana said it was less trouble to do it themselves, and then they felt ashamed, and feeling ashamed made them more cross than ever. The truth was they were all tired, and badly in need of a change of air. On Petrova's birthday they had made their vows in the sitting-room after tea.

"We three Fossils vow to try and put our name into history books, because it's our very own, and nobody can say it's because of our grandfathers, and we vow to try and earn money for Garnie until Gum comes home."

Petrova held up her right arm.

"We vow," she said.

They both looked at Posy.

"What happened to the 'Amen'?" Posy whispered because she did not want to interrupt the vowing.

"Go on, vow," Petrova hissed at her.

Posy held up her arm.

"We vow."

Then suddenly she burst into tears.

Pauline and Petrova stared at her.

"What on earth's the matter?" Pauline asked.

"Last year you said 'Amen'," Posy wailed, "and it brought us luck; we had pocket money and I went and saw the ballet; and now everything's so miserable, and I thought if we said 'Amen' again everything might come right."

Petrova went to the window and looked out. Cromwell Road was looking hot and dusty; there was nothing to do except go for walks, because there was only just enough money for necessities. Certainly everything was miserable, and it was her birthday which made it worse. A lump came into her throat, and before she could stop them tears began to drip off her nose.

"Oh, for goodness' sake don't you cry too!" Pauline gulped, for she was not feeling at all cheerful herself. "I still might get the film."

The other two did not answer to that, not wanting to be unkind, but they were both sure somebody else had been engaged long ago. Instead they sobbed. Pauline looked first at one and then at the other, then suddenly she ran out of the room and slammed the door. She raced down to the drawing-room.

"Garnie," she said, jumping on to the arm of the chair in which Sylvia was sitting in front of her desk, "can I take my money out of the savings bank and buy a little tent and the three of us go and camp for a week?"

"But you can't camp alone," Sylvia protested.

"No, but we could on the Common next to the doctors, because it's free to camp, and then my money would pay for a room as well at the little inn, and you could come one week, and Nana the other; we could be fetched very quickly from there for an audition."

"All your savings?" Sylvia looked worried. "I don't like it."

"We need a holiday," Pauline said firmly. "The other two are crying."

"What about?"

"Just nothing."

"Well, that certainly does sound like needing a holiday," Sylvia agreed. "Where's Nana?"

"Washing in the bathroom—shall I fetch her?"

Nana entirely approved of the idea, but she absolutely refused to have a week at the inn herself.

"I'll stop here, dear," she said to Sylvia; "you go down—you haven't been away in years. I'll go to my sister's for a day or two when you get back."

It was surprising how cheerful they all became the moment the holiday was decided. They sent a prepaid telegram to the doctors asking if they could book them a camp, and got a reply in an hour and a half, saying: "Splendid! Will arrange everything".

The next morning Pauline applied at the post office to draw out her savings. Sylvia wanted her to take out only ten pounds as a start, but she said "No; she'd promise to put back anything that was over." They thought they would have to wait three days after that before they could buy the tent, but Clara said she had ten pounds and would lend it. In the wildest excitement they went out and bought a tent and a ground sheet, and stuff for three palliasses. They gave Nana and Sylvia the stuff, and then went out again and bought shorts and shirts. When they came in, one of the palliasses was done, and Clara and Nana were working on the other two, while Sylvia looked for suitable blankets and pillows.

Two days later they arrived on the Common. The doctors had arranged to have Sylvia in the cottage, and had got permission from a farmer for the girls to camp in a field of a farm near by. They had fixed that they should come every day for their middle-day meal at the cottage, for which Pauline was to pay a pound a week. For breakfast, tea, and supper they were to cook and cater for themselves.

Perhaps it was because they were not expecting a holiday at all, or perhaps because it was Pauline's holiday which she had paid for, but there was not one second which they did not find perfect. They took turns to cook, and it was lovely waking in the mornings to hear the cows mooing, and the cocks crowing, and to turn over and prod the day's cook to get up and deal with breakfast. The palliasses stuffed with straw they found gloriously comfortable, and it was the height of luxury to lie on them sniffing the first smoke of the fire through the open flap of the tent before jumping up to race down to the stream in a bathing dress for a wash before breakfast.

The food varied a lot with who was cooking and catering. Eggs were the easiest things for breakfast, because they bought them from the farm; but for supper they had all sorts of things—sausages when Petrova was in charge, and two courses at least from Pauline. When Posy was catering, a great deal of cake got into the menu.

The weather was not too good, but the farmer lent them a large barn for wet days, in which they practiced every morning, wet or fine, as they had, of course, their ballet shoes with them; here, when it rained, they played a new and glorious kind of hide-and-seek. It consisted in the hiders burying themselves in the straw, which the nervous seeker had to prod. If the hider could grab any part of the seeker, she won; but if the seeker could see a movement in the hay, and lay a hand on the place, and say "One of you is here," then she won. The game was such a thrilling one that when it was wet Sylvia and the two doctors usually came and played too.

Just before they were due to go home, Nana sent Sylvia a telegram. Pauline was to be taken to the studio; she was to play Henrietta.

Pauline's picture relieved financial worry for the time being. She was engaged at ten pounds a day, with a minimum of ten days' work. Even allowing for ten pounds of that belonging to the Academy, ninety were for the house and clothes. They planned to start shooting the picture by the end of September or the beginning of October; but Pauline learned that films were a different matter from plays. For a play they said rehearsals would begin next Monday, and they began next Monday; but with a film, weeks could go by between the day they expected to start and the day they actually began.

She was called to fittings for clothes throughout September, and very exciting she found it, as they were the most beautiful she had ever had—simple, of course, for a child, but most beautifully made and embroidered. In spite of the fact that her clothes had been finished for weeks, it was not until the last week in October that she was called to the studio.

Pauline had spent such time as she was free from the Academy and from working for her school certificate, which she was taking in the spring, in studying books on Charles the Second, and reading all she could find about Henrietta. She came to work at the studios with the same strong feeling of being out of herself, and into another person that she had with "King Edward". She had been discouraged by the script the studio had sent her; the speeches were short, and she was confused by the way the scenes were divided into "takes"; they seemed to her so short that it would be difficult to sustain the part when everything was broken up.

When she came on the floor for her first day's work she grasped that this was a new technique; it was not doing stage acting in front of the camera: it was doing film acting, which was a totally different thing. She loathed it, she loathed the hours of hanging about, the endless rehearsals before a scene was right, and the still more innumerable "takes" before it would pass for cameras and sound.

One day she was called for a small scene played between herself and Charles the Second. Charles was a film actor known all over the world, an Englishman who had made his name in Hollywood. The scene was before a journey of his to England, in which he begged his little sister to write. She had to say that she would try, and he had to take her chin in his hands and say: "Not 'I will try,' Minette, but 'I will'." Then he had to look away and say almost under his breath: "Mine is a lonely road, little sister." They rehearsed for nearly two hours, and then they began the "takes". Mr. Sholsky mopped his forehead. The boy with the board came forward. " 'Charles the Exile. Director, Mr. Sholsky. Camera, Mr. Rosenblaum. Sound, Mr. Benjamin. Scene 84. Take one'." The lights were all on, the cameras whirring. The boy clacked the clappers. "Oh, how boring this is!" thought Pauline. "Action," said Mr. Sholsky. They played the tiny scene. Charles turned away. "Mine is a lonely road, little sister." She looked at him as directed, and was amazed; after rehearsing so long, and in spite of the scene being so short, his eyes were full of tears. After the "take" Mr. Sholsky came over to her.

"You got a look in your face when you looked up at Charles, that was the first sign you've given me that you aren't made of wood."

"That was him," Pauline explained. "When I looked at him, he was almost crying."

Mr. Sholsky caught both her hands in his.

"That man can act for the pictures. You've been holding out on me since the shooting began because a lot of cock-eyed critics gave you a write-up as the Prince in the Tower. Well, forget it. You've everything to learn in motion pictures; today watching Charles you saw something real. Well, you can do that too; let's have it from you."

Pauline told nobody what Mr. Sholsky had said. When Sylvia, who came down to the studio with her every day, asked her what he had been saying, she answered vaguely it was about the part; but from that moment she found the work far less tedious, and sometimes, for a moment or two, she was able to feel not Pauline, but Princess Henrietta.

Sylvia sold the house; it was to be part of a hotel, and the purchaser would take it over on the June quarter day of next year. Petrova, knowing how often she had cried at the thought of the house going, was very sorry for the others; but she wasted her sympathy, for neither of them cared as she did. Pauline was too busy at the studio, and Posy too wrapped up in her dancing.

That Christmas, Pauline was engaged for the Fairy-Godmother in a pantomime of "Cinderella", and Petrova was one of twenty-four jumping beans, who were to do specialty dances in "Jack and the Beanstalk" in a theater in the suburbs.

Pauline's film was finished, and there was no suggestion of using her for another, so she was glad to get the Fairy Godmother, though she found the words she had to say terrible rubbish. Petrova and Posy thought her part an awful joke. They quoted it endlessly: " 'Oh Cinders, Cinders, do not fear. Your Fairy Godmother is here'," Posy said on bursting into the bathroom while Pauline was in the bath. Or Petrova recited when she saw her start off to her rehearsal: " 'If after twelve you should delay. Your glories all will pass away'." Pauline did not care how much they laughed, she had the most lovely fairy dress for the transformation scene, and rather a nice solo dance to do. Nana was entranced by her dress.

"That's more like it," she said, "white and silver tissue, and nice wings and a wand—nothing could be prettier. That's better than those high-brow combinations."

Sylvia or Nana took her to her rehearsals, and fetched her again for lunch, and after work was over for the day; she was just fifteen, and they thought they could trust her to look after herself. It made her feel very grown-up, and she enjoyed it.

Petrova thought being a jumping bean the worst

thing that had happened to her. The twenty-four beans were taken to rehearsals by a matron, Mrs. Brick. She was a nice woman, but strict. She made all the children walk two and two, and she expected them to be very quiet on the underground, and she liked them to get into their shoes and practice-rompers the second they reached the theater, and if she could, would have marched them on to the stage as though they were soldiers. When they were not wanted on the stage she liked them to work at their exercises, as she said "Satan found . . ."

They were too far away to get back to the Academy for tea, so they had it in the dressing-room before they went home, and just before the production, after the school holidays had started, they had a sandwich lunch there as well, with what Mrs. Brick called "a nice brisk walk" afterwards. A nice brisk walk meant that they all had to change back into their outdoor things and, two and two, walk rapidly four times round the big square outside. She thought that it was dull for children to hang about with nothing to do when they were neither wanted nor practicing, so she brought games for them to play, and books which she read out loud to them. The other twenty-three girls loved Mrs. Brick, and enjoyed being read to, and playing Happy Families; but Petrova had one of her mechanical handbooks always with her, and she longed for any corner where she could get away in peace and quiet to study it. Actually, if she had explained what she wanted to Mrs. Brick, it would have been arranged for her; but she never did, and so she spent her free time during rehearsals, and in between the matinée and evening performances, after the run had started, listening to books being read out loud which she did not like, and playing games she did not want to play. Mr. Simpson was the person who appreciated how she must feel.

"Pretty boring that jumping bean stuff, isn't it?" he said.

Petrova made a face.

"Simply disgusting."

"Must be. I've fixed up for us to go up from Stag Lane on Sunday."

The worst of it was that the nicer, and more understanding, Mr. Simpson was, the worse it seemed that after June he would be living somewhere else.

"I don't see how I'll bear it after you've gone," she told him.

"Cheer up," he said. "We'll still be able to have our Sundays. Besides, time's getting on; in three and a half years you can learn to be a chauffeur."

It had been hoped that both pantomimes would

run over February, but the death of King George in January cut the audiences down to about a quarter for the week following his death, and they never really pulled up again. Nobody felt in the mood for pantomimes. Pauline's did run to the end of February, but Petrova's came off at the end of January; she tried to feel sorry because of the money, but she was earning very little, and simply could not help being glad really.

In the middle of March Posy came home from the Academy with her face swollen from crying. Madame had been taken suddenly ill; she had to go to Switzerland for a cure and it might be months before she was back.

"Oh, poor Madame!" said Sylvia.

Posy turned on her.

"Madame! I'm not thinking of her; it's my training, it ought not to be broken off now."

XVIII

Posy

*

Posy was in disgrace. Sylvia and Nana were horrified to find her, as they considered, selfish and hard-hearted. It was all very well to be ambitious, but ambition should not kill the nice qualities in you.

Pauline and Petrova discussed Posy together. It was a Sunday, and they were walking to church.

"You know," Pauline said, "everybody at home and at the Academy is shocked at Posy; but I think I know why she's being awful about Madame."

Petrova looked surprised.

"But of course it's because of her being twelve in September. Madame has left the dancing school in charge of Theo. Theo's nice, but she's not a dancer in the way Posy thinks of dancing."

"Do you suppose"—Pauline lowered her voice, for Sylvia and Posy were catching up with them—"that Madame hasn't said what's to happen when Posy's twelve? She wouldn't want her to go into a dancing troupe or anything like that."

Petrova looked round to see that Posy was out of whisper-shot.

"Madame was very ill when she went—much iller than people know, Theo told me—but you mustn't tell anybody else. She's going to get quite all right, but it will take months. They didn't want to fuss Posy saying how bad she was, and so they made her sound only a little ill; that's why Posy's so cross—she can't understand Madame, after all she has said, going off without a word, leaving no directions for what's to happen to her."

"It is awful for her," Pauline said sympathetically.

The Academy lost patience with Posy. It was bad enough to have Madame away ill, without her making things worse by being difficult. Sylvia and Nana had decided that it would be good for her to go to the ordinary dancing classes with the rest of the school, that a child of her age was not to be allowed to dictate what she would, or would not, do.

"It's no good sending me to the Academy half the day," Posy explained. "There's nothing for me to do except have a French lesson, and practice, and I can do both those at home."

But at home special lessons were being given to Pauline, as she was sitting for her school certificate that summer, and whoever was not attending to her taught

Petrova; it was not a good moment to change the plans and put Posy's full education back on the doctors. Sylvia taught her for a bit in the afternoon to make up for the hours in which she had learnt Spanish and Russian with Madame—not that she had ever seemed to learn either language, but she had studied them.

Sylvia had a talk with Theo about her; it was planned that she should do four and a half hours' lessons at home, and her half-hour of French with Madame Moulin at the Academy; but that after that she was to join the senior ballet class for an hour whether she liked it or not, and then she should practice on her own in Madame's room until Pauline and Petrova were ready to go home. Posy was furious, protesting that an hour's ballet class with the seniors was the most ridiculous waste of time, as she had been doing more advanced work than they did for over a year. But Sylvia was firm.

"I expect there's a lot you can learn; you've too good an opinion of yourself."

Madame Moulin, at her French lesson, heard her grumbles about waste of time, and told her the story of the old French actress that she had told Pauline. Posy was not impressed as Pauline had been.

"It's all very well," she said, "for an actress to *n'oubliez jamais* that she can continue *à apprendre jusqu'à son dernier jour*. But it's silly for a dancer. She'd much better *n'oubliez jamais* that you can't be a first-class dancer for very many years, and that all her *apprendre*-ing would have to be done while she was still young."

Madame Moulin laughed and patted her cheek, and said she was an *enfant terrible*. "*Mais tu me fais rire.*"

For two or three days Posy attended her dancing class and did what she was told; but with so little energy that none of the exercises were any good to her. Then one day she bounded into the class looking radiant. She took her place at the bar. Theo came to the middle of the room.

"Place your left hands on the bar," she directed. "Battement serré, fifty times; then right hands on the bar, fifty more on the other foot."

She gave a nod at the pianist, and the class rose on their left points and began work.

Theo walked to the far end of the room, and closely studied each girl. Then she was distracted by giggles, and went to see what was wrong. As soon as she arrived the girls tried to straighten their faces, but they were not all able to. Theo looked round for the cause of the joke, but she could see nothing; all those who were laughing were on the bar immediately behind Posy, but she had not a glimmer of a smile on her face, and was working beautifully. Theo turned away, and as she did so, the first fifty Battements finished, and all the class reversed, and held the bar with their right hands, and stood on their right points. Once more there came smothered laughter, but this time it was from a different lot of girls. Theo made no comment; but she knew that the culprit must be Posy, from the fact that each time the laughter came from the girls immediately behind her, whether she faced left or right. Theo could see nothing wrong; nobody in the class was working harder than Posy, and the expression on her face was positively angelic.

From that moment the senior class went to pieces; they were always laughing and watching Posy. After a day or two Theo realized why. Posy, though she did what she was told, never did the exercises as herself, but in imitation of some well-known figure in the Academy. It was incredible how, with nothing in the way of properties, she managed to give such realistic impersonations. One day she was Madame Moulin, with all her French mannerisms incorporated into the exercises, and another time she was Smithy, the cook-housekeeper in charge of the refectory. Smithy had great trouble with corns, and a habit of smoothing her apron over her hips, Posy doing Fouetté as though she had corns would have made anyone laugh. In the end there was nobody in the Academy who had peculiarities, whom Posy did not imitate.

Theo bore with her for a bit; she did not want to worry Sylvia, who she knew was up to her eyes with work to do with selling the house. In the end she went to Pauline, and told her how naughty Posy was being, and how it was impossible to teach a class with her in it, and asked her if she would try having a talk with her.

Pauline knew it was no good having a talk with Posy, who had always said the senior ballet class was a waste of time for her, and who would consider, if she was made to attend it in spite of what she said, that she had a right to do what she liked during it. Pauline also knew what fun it must be for Posy to pass the time doing imitations; she always loved doing them, and the sort of audience she would get at the senior ballet class would be just the sort she would adore.

Posy was having her bath as Pauline came in.

"The Marmaro Ballet is coming over in May, did you know?"

Posy's face lit up.

"Of course I did. Manoff is coming here for the first time since he danced here in the Diaghileff ballets before the war."

"Is he good?"

"Good!" Posy looked scornful. "He's much more than good. Ever since nineteen-twenty, when he founded his school in Czechoslovakia, he has worked and worked. People go in hundreds to see him over there, but this is the first year he has thought his ballet fit to show the world. Imagine it! Some of his students who are now dancing for him came to him as little as we were when we went to the Academy."

"Would you like to see him dance?"

"Would I!" Posy soaped her neck gloomily. "I'd rather see him dance than anything else in the world. He is only dancing in 'Petroushka'. They say his 'Petroushka' is the finest there has ever been. But I can't go without any money."

Pauline sat on the edge of the bath.

"I've got two pounds. I put what was over of my savings back in the post office after our camp, but Garnie made me take two pounds out of my film money. If you will work properly at your ballet class with Theo, I'll buy seats, one for you, and one for someone to take you, to see 'Petroushka'."

Posy jumped out of the bath and threw her very soapy arms round Pauline.

"Pauline, you wouldn't. I'll work and work and

work, however silly they all are. Could it be the circle, so that I can see the feet?"

"It could." Pauline pushed Posy back into the bath. "You're making me wet. I won't get the seats yet though, and only if Theo says you've been so good you couldn't be gooder."

Posy carefully washed her left ear.

"You can buy them at once quite safely, I'm certain to be an angel with a bribe like that. Oh, Pauline . . ." she got out of the bath—"this is Theo doing 'Pas de chat' with her back to the class and trying not to pretend that she's wanting to look round to see if anyone's laughing at me."

Pauline tried to frown, but she could not. Posy, even with nothing on, and dripping with water, was quite amazingly like Theo. She leaned against the door and laughed.

The accounts of Posy's behavior were so good that the moment the dates of the Marmaro Ballet were published she bought two seats in the middle of the front row of the dress circle. They were for Wednesday, May the twentieth. Posy was told she could invite any grown-up she liked for the other seat, and she at once chose Sylvia.

Two days after Pauline had bought the ballet seats, she got a large envelope at breakfast. In it were seats

for the première of "Charles the Exile", one for herself, and two for friends. The date was Wednesday,
May the twentieth. She was very worried what to do,
but Sylvia settled the point.

"I'll take Posy to her ballet as arranged," she said.
"You take Petrova and Nana to your première. I can
go and see the film later on, when we're settled in a
flat. It's sure to be shown everywhere presently."

Although they were leaving the house on the
twenty-fourth of the next month, Sylvia had not
found a flat. It was difficult to find one big enough
for five people that was not too expensive. All the
cheaper ones were so far away from the Academy that
if she took one it would cost such a lot to get them all
to and fro each day. Theo was provided for, because
she was taking over Madame's flat near the Academy;
she was only going to use a bedroom, but she would
see that the rest of it was kept in order. Mr. and Mrs.
Simpson had booked a furnished flat for a month near
Selfridge's, and said they should find a permanent
home in the autumn. Cook and Clara planned to take
a good holiday before going to new situations. The
doctors had found a very charming flat in Bloomsbury;
it was not far from the Academy, which they said
would make it very convenient for the girls' lessons.

It was rather a miserable Spring. They all hated

the feeling of their home being broken up. None of the boarders wanted to move, and though Sylvia was thankful for the money, she found the trials of flat-hunting most depressing. They were glad when it came to the twentieth, and, as Nana said, "An outing would do them all good."

By dint of buying some extra organdie and letting out, and adding some frills, Nana had succeeded in making the frocks Pauline and Petrova had bought for "A Midsummer Night's Dream" audition do for Petrova and Posy. Pauline had a new frock. She was fifteen and a half, and though very small for her age, too old for frills and sashes. Had the matter of what she should wear been left to Nana to decide, she would probably have managed to have let out Pauline's organdie sufficiently for her to wear it, and sent Posy to the ballet in the black chiffon velvet which had now passed down to her, but Pauline had a film agent.

Mr. Ben Reubens had been to see the trade show of "Charles the Exile", and had at once got in touch with the Academy, and through them with Sylvia. He had been to see Sylvia, and had taken Pauline on his list. His list of film stars for whom he did business, he told Sylvia, was the greatest in the world. He asked if Pauline was going to the première, and on hearing that she was, he had held up a finger warningly.

"Young, but not too young. Let her look her age."

Because of Mr. Reubens' words—and he seemed a man who knew what he was talking about—Sylvia bought a "Vogue", and after consultation with Nana and Pauline, several yards of blue taffeta and blue organdie. The frock that Nana made was a triumph. It was much longer than anything Pauline had worn before, and made her look quite sixteen, she thought, though, as a matter of fact, she still appeared younger than she was. But she looked perfectly lovely in it, and Nana was bursting with pride.

Mr. Simpson drove them to the Cinema. The picture was not shown till nine, and Sylvia and Posy had gone on the underground to the ballet an hour before. There was the most enormous crowd outside the Cinema House, all waiting to see film stars go in and to get their autographs. Mr. Simpson had to put them down quite a long way from the Cinema. Nana put Pauline and Petrova behind her, and pushed her way to the entrance saying "If you please", and "Excuse me". In the foyer were lots more people, all in evening dress, and cameras taking their photographs. Of course nobody was interested in Pauline or Petrova, so they were able to look about, and there was plenty to see. All round the walls were men dressed as people were dressed in the reign of Charles the Second, and there were "stills" from the film in large frames.

Their seats were in the circle—very nice ones—and they were pleased to find that the programs were free. They were very grand programs—large, with bows on them, and a photograph of Charles the Second on the front. Inside was a synopsis of the story, which they read—even Pauline. There were photographs of the leading actors, and a list, in very large print, of all the people who had made the picture. On the next page, in the same sized letters, were the stars of the cast, and, in smaller letters, the rest of the actors. Pauline had not a photograph in the program, and her name was in small letters. Petrova said she thought it was mean: that as Charles the Second's sister she ought to have her name printed large; but Pauline pointed out that even in the size she was printed, her name was bigger than the author's, and in sympathizing with the smallness of his print, they forgot to think any more about hers.

The film was a great success. Pauline looked lovely, and came across very well on the screen. They were delighted with the evening, because as well as the big film there was a news reel, and a very good Mickey Mouse, which, as Nana said, was giving a lot for nothing.

They hung back after the show to get away from
the worst of the crowd, and even then, when they
came down the stairs and into the street, there were
masses of people standing about. Pauline looked round
for a gap of them to get through, and it was then it
happened. A voice said: "There she is. That's Pauline
Fossil." In one second the crowd seemed to fall on her,
people waved books and bits of paper at her, and shoved
pencils into her hand. She gave Nana a scared look, but
Nana was equal to the occasion.

"Lot of silly women, dear," she whispered. "If
they're foolish enough to want your autograph, give it
to them."

Pauline signed and signed until her hand ached,
and then, just as she thought she could not bear it any
more, Nana did a most unexpected thing. She caught
a policeman by the arm.

"Constable," she said, "it's time we were home,
would you get us into a taxi?"

He was a splendid policeman. In one moment he
seemed to find a taxi, push Nana and Petrova into it,
and lift Pauline over the heads of the crowd and put
her in after them. Then he saluted and slammed the
door.

They all sat silent for quite a long time, they were
so surprised, and both the girls rather scared by what

had happened. Then Petrova thought of the policeman.

"What a lovely man that was," she said.

"Nana"—Pauline leant against her—"why was it? They didn't when we went in."

"The film, dear," Nana explained. "You must have made a hit."

Pauline looked puzzled.

"But why? I wasn't very good. Not nearly as good as I was as 'Edward', and there wasn't all that fuss then."

Nana patted her hand.

"Don't you think any more about it. Lot of hysterical idiots, that's what they were. They don't know good from bad."

Posy came back from the ballet very silent, and went to bed almost without a word. Pauline woke with a jump soon after she had gone to sleep, and saw her standing by the window.

"Posy!" she whispered. "What is it?"

"Manoff." Posy's voice was queer and high-pitched. "I've got to learn from him, Pauline—I must."

Pauline yawned.

"But he teaches in Czechoslovakia."

Posy, however, was beyond reason; she was almost in tears.

"I must learn from him."

Pauline got out of bed, took her by the arm, put her into her bed, and tucked her in.

"Don't let's argue about it," she said comfortingly. "You won't make it easier to learn from him by getting up in the middle of the night. I should get to sleep."

She got back into her own bed, and managed to stay awake until she heard, by Posy's breathing, she had done what she suggested. Then she turned over, and settled down herself. Her last thought was of sheets of paper and pencils.

"Silly idiots!" she murmured.

XIX

Gum Comes Back

*

IT WAS at lessons the next morning that they discovered Posy was missing; she had been at breakfast, but no one had seen her since. Doctor Jakes and Doctor Smith went outside, and discussed what was best to be done, and when they came back they told Pauline and Petrova not to say anything to Nana or Sylvia yet, that even if they rang up the police nothing would be done for an hour or two, and by that time Posy might be back. She was almost twelve, and unlikely to get run over.

They began lessons, but they were very unusual ones. Every time there was a noise on the stairs, both doors shot open, and Doctor Jakes's and Pauline's head came out of one, and Doctor Smith's and Petrova's out of the other. "Is that you, Posy?" they all said. It never was. They were glad when it came to beaver time; but although there was a plate of strawberry ice each, none of them had the heart to eat it, and they looked unhappily at the bit left in the box, which was Posy's share.

In the middle of the morning Clara came up, and told Pauline she was wanted in the drawing-room.

"Why?" Pauline asked.

Clara looked mysterious.

"That Mr. Reubens is here with Miss Brown, and from what I heard it might be good news."

Pauline's going made the doctors decide not to struggle with any more lessons; it was a farce, anyway, for they were none of them thinking of work, but only of Posy.

Petrova sat on the bottom step of the stairs, where she could watch the front door. She could hear voices in the drawing-room: Mr. Reubens' deep one, and Sylvia's high one, and quite a lot of Pauline's. She could not hear what they were saying, but just voices. Presently the drawing-room door opened and Pauline came out. She looked rather odd. She came to the stairs and shared Petrova's step.

"Posy back?"

"No."

"He"—Pauline nodded in the direction of Mr. Reubens, "has been offered a lot of money for me to go to Hollywood."

"Goodness!" said Petrova. "Does he want to make you a film star?"

"Yes." Pauline put her elbows on her knees, and

rested her chin in her hands. "But I don't want to be."

"Why not?"

"I want to be an actress," Pauline explained: "an actress on the stage. It's quite different from pictures."

"How much money would they pay you?"

Pauline looked embarrassed.

"You wouldn't believe it, but about a hundred pounds a week, perhaps more, because the English studio want me to stay here. Mr. Reubens says that the English studio didn't realize that America would want me, or they'd have had me under contract."

"Goodness!" Petrova gazed at her. "A hundred pounds a week!"

"More, quite likely." Pauline hugged her knees. "But I don't want to go; it's for five years, or it could be, if they take up their options."

"Five years!" Petrova stared at her horrified. "Would you go all alone?"

"No, Garnie would come too."

Petrova opened her eyes.

"Then what about us?"

Pauline shrugged her shoulders.

"I don't know. Garnie said if I wanted to go, it could be arranged."

"Did you say you wouldn't go?"

"Yes." Pauline frowned. "But Mr. Reubens said I

was to come out and talk it over with both of you."

"You can't talk it over with Posy," Petrova said sadly. "I do wish she would come back."

She had hardly said the words when the front door opened and in burst Posy, with her attaché case in her hand.

"Posy! Where have you been?" the other two asked together.

Posy did not answer that, but joined them at the bottom of the stairs.

"He'll take me," she said in an ecstatic voice.

"Who?" asked Petrova.

Pauline remembered last night.

"Monsieur Manoff?"

Posy clasped her hands.

"Yes. Isn't it just the most wonderful thing that has ever happened? I went out to the theater, and I was lucky; there was a rehearsal, and the ballet were going in. They none of them spoke English, but just said something funny to the doorkeeper, which I suppose was good morning. I saw he didn't know any of them by sight, so I walked in too, and just said 'Beaver-time,' which might be Czechoslovakian for good morning. I went down on the stage, and put on my ballet shoes. Presently the ballet came down. Nobody said anything to me. Then Monsieur Manoff came. There was a most terrific bowing and curtsying; they call him 'Maître'. Of course I curtsied too. Then he saw me. He came over, and asked what I wanted, and I told him that he should see me dance; and he said not then, there was a rehearsal; but I said it would be a mistake not to see me, and I couldn't wait. So he laughed and called me to the middle of the stage. Then he gave directions. You cannot imagine . . ." Posy got up, and gave an imitation of Manoff giving directions at great speed, and herself trying to follow, but always a bit late. "At the end he asked who had taught me, and when I told him, he blew a kiss and said, 'I understand now'. Then he said, 'You will come to me to Szolyva'—that's where the school is—'and I will make you into a beautiful artiste'. So I said I would get Garnie to make the arrangements, and I came home."

"But, Posy," Petrova gasped, "how do you think Garnie is going to afford to send you there? In any case, you're a child—you can't go alone."

"No, I thought of that," Posy agreed. "Nana will have to live there with me, or Garnie."

"But what about money?" Petrova insisted.

Posy's face grew anxious.

"She'll have to get it." She clasped the end of the banisters. "I must go. I must."

"But you can't." Petrova caught hold of her. "It's silly to pretend you can, Posy; Garnie hasn't any money—you know that. You must get it into your head. You can't go."

Pauline got up.

"Yes, you can, Posy; wait a second." She went into the drawing-room. She was out again in a few minutes.

"That's settled. Garnie's signing for me now." She looked rather miserably round the hall. "Imagine five years!" She turned to Posy. "It will be all right for you; I shall pay—I'm going to make an awful lot of money: enough to keep you, and Nana, in Czechoslovakia, as well as Garnie and me in Hollywood."

"Oh! Pauline darling." Posy flung her arms round her neck, then jumped up and pirouetted round the hall.

Petrova tried not to feel selfish, but it was rather tremblingly that she said to Pauline:

"What about me?"

"You!" Pauline considered her. "I don't know. We didn't talk about you."

"No, I suppose not," Petrova agreed, and tried not to cry. To prevent herself she changed the subject. "That'll put an end to our vowing—at least, we can't do it all together."

Posy stopped in the middle of a pirouette.

"We couldn't vow any more, anyhow."

Pauline nodded.

"No."

Petrova looked puzzled.

"Why not?"

Posy came to her and leant her hands on her knees. "Did you ever read of a dancer in a history book?"

"Or a film star?" asked Pauline.

"No, I suppose not," Petrova agreed. "But . . ."

Pauline looked at Posy and nodded.

"That's an idea."

"What is?" said Petrova.

"You." Posy turned a cartwheel. "You'll go into history books. That'll put Fossil there all right; it doesn't matter about Pauline and me."

Petrova looked puzzled.

"How will I?"

"Flying, of course." Posy, who was still very excited after her interview with Manoff, turned another cartwheel.

"Would that?" said Petrova.

"Of course." Pauline spoke eagerly. "Don't you see? It's sort of exploring, like Frobisher, or Drake. Amy Mollison and Jean Batten will be there, but not as important as you. The books will say: 'The greatest

explorer in the middle of the twentieth century was
Petrova Fossil, who found routes by which goods could
be carried at greater speed and less cost, and so she
revolutionized trade.' Come here, Posy, and stop showing off." Posy came to her. "This is the vow you and
I must make on our birthdays—Petrova can make the
old one—'I vow to help in any way I can to put Petrova into history books, because her name is Fossil,
and it's our very own, and nobody can say it's because
of our Grandfathers.' I'll write it out for you, or you'll
forget it."

"No, I won't. I'll learn it with my feet, and then
I'll know it always." Posy got up, and walked out a
routine of steps, then she walked them again, then did
them faster.

"Fancy," Petrova said, "me. You'd think I'd be
the one to do nothing at all."

Pauline shook her head.

"I wouldn't. I've always thought you were the one
that might. Film stars and dancers are nice things to
be, but they aren't important."

Posy had learnt the vow with her feet, and she spun
round the hall. At that moment the door opened.

The man who came in was old; he had a gray
beard, a wooden leg, and a shabby hold-all in one

hand. Posy stopped dancing. Pauline and Petrova stood up, and then, as if the old man was a magnet, they were drawn down the hall toward him.

The old man plunked his suitcase on the floor, and looked round at the girls in an irritated way.

"It's always the same," he said. "I keep a pack of women in this house, and they're never about when they're wanted."

"Is it possible," Pauline asked politely, "that you are Gum?"

"Gum! Of course I'm Gum. Who else should I be? Who're you?"

"Pauline."

"Petrova."

"Posy."

He stared at them.

"But you were babies. I collected babies."

Posy patted his arm comfortingly.

"You've been away some time, you know."

"Some time? I suppose I have. One forgets. Well, let's sit down and hear all about you."

They sat round him on the stairs, because there was nowhere else where they could all sit. They told him everything: about how poor they had been, and the house being sold, and finally the day's news.

"I'm going with Garnie to Hollywood to be a film star," Pauline explained.

Posy thumped his good knee.

"And I'm going with Nana to Czechoslovakia to train under Manoff."

Gum swung round and looked at Petrova.

"That seems to leave you and me. What would you like to do?"

"Flying and motor cars," Posy put in, before Petrova could answer.

"That suits me." Gum looked pleased. "I'd like to fly—get about quickly. There are lots of things you can pick up if you get about quickly. Cook and Clara still here?" They told him they were. "Good! Then they shall look after us, as you're taking Sylvia and Nana. Might hire a car tomorrow, Petrova, and find a house near an aerodrome where you could study." He got up. "Where's Sylvia?"

"In there." Pauline pointed to the drawing-room. "But you'd better not go in, she's signing my contract. Mr. Reubens is there."

"Think I care for contracts or Mr. Reubens?" Gum opened the drawing-room door and hobbled in.

The three girls stared after him. Pauline smiled.

"He's nice."

"I'd like to live with him if I wasn't going to Czechoslovakia," said Posy.

"I shall like it." Petrova looked radiant. A house near an aerodrome. Gum, Cook, Clara. It did sound fun.

"What different things we are going to do!" said Pauline.

"In such different places," added Posy.

"I wonder"—Petrova looked up—"if other girls had to be one of us, which of us they'd choose to be?"

the Judy Blume Diary

The Place to Put Your Own Feelings

This diary is wonderfully different from most because it can be started on any day of any year. It's a <u>special place</u> to write about your own <u>special feelings</u>. Spiral-bound, THE JUDY BLUME DIARY features a letter from the author, quotations from her books, and 36 black-and-white photographs.

Like your thoughts, THE JUDY BLUME DIARY belongs to you. It's the place to put your own feelings, whenever and however you like.

YEARLING $6.95

LLOYD ALEXANDER

THE PRYDAIN CHRONICLES

These fantasy classics follow Assistant Pig-Keeper Taran and his companions through many magical adventures in their struggle against the evil Lord of Death. The five-book series is packed with action, humor, and gallantry that will keep readers of all ages coming back for more.